BYCATCH

A Novel

ALEXANDER BLEVENS

Relax. Read. Repeat.

To Nancy

12/22/22

Biloxi, MS

BYCATCH
By Alexander Blevens
Published by TouchPoint Press
Brookland, AR 72417
www.touchpointpress.com

PAPERBACK ISBN: 978-1-956851-23-6

Editor: Kimberly Coghlan
Cover Design: DL Havlin and ColbieMyles.com
Cover Image: Adobe Stock

First Edition

Printed in the United States of America.

To my father.

"Life is the sum of your choices."
-Albert Camus

Your children are not your children.
They are the sons and daughters of Life's longing for itself.
They come through you but not from you,
And though they are with you, yet they belong not to you.
-Kahlil Gibran

"By·catch" *noun*\ˈbī-ˌkach, -ˌkech\: the portion of a commercial fishing catch that consists of marine animals caught unintentionally.
-Webster's Third New International Dictionary, Unabridged.

CHAPTER 1

Biloxi, Mississippi, August 16, 1993

Wooden blades slapped the dark, still water, pulling a flat-bottomed skiff across the Biloxi Bay. Jake crouched low at the bow and trained his eyes on a lone white light ahead. His younger brother Pigeon worked the oars. Both were in their early twenties, lean and muscular. A single black skimmer glided over the water, beating its wings past the boat through the summer's thick, humid air. No moon or stars filled the midnight sky, just as the brothers had hoped. They had a task to do, a score to settle.

At the far end of the bay, six hundred yards off Deer Island, a trawler rested at anchor. From its boom, a bright halogen beam lit up huge nets hanging from outriggers on either side of the vessel. With forty-two feet at the waterline, she had the classic, graceful lines of a Gulf Coast shrimper. Across the transom and bow, the name *Miss Anh* arched in newly gilded letters. Her gold nameboard, green pilothouse, and red hull presented a semblance of Christmas.

Jake felt the gentle vibration of an electric generator as he grabbed the trawler's anchor line to steady the skiff. Without a sound, Pigeon stowed the oars and pulled on heavy knit gloves. He dragged a canvas sack from beneath his seat and gave it to Jake. Sweat beaded on Pigeon's brow and ran into the corners of his eyes. He eased himself over the skiff's gunwale and into the warm bay. Jake pulled a length of cable—looped at each end—out of the sack. Holding on to one end of the coil, he handed the remainder over the side. For a moment, the heavy wire dragged Pigeon's head underwater.

"Gimme that float," Pigeon mouthed as he struggled at the surface.

Jake tossed a square white seat cushion to his brother. Pigeon trapped the pad under his arm then played out the cable with one hand as he side-kicked along the hull of the *Miss Anh*. At the stern, he grabbed a tire bumper hanging from the back rail to rest a moment. Looking up to the transom and the new golden letters, he mumbled, "Those bastards." Then he took a deep breath, released the cushion, and sank into the inky water.

The brothers had been raised on the Mississippi Gulf Coast since they were teenagers and had spent most of their days helping their father run this same boat. They knew every cleat and line, every block and winch, and every seam of its wooden hull.

The free end of the cable pulled on Pigeon's arm as he made his way, by memory and feel, down six feet to the propeller. In the darkness, he guided the wire loop around the prop shaft and over one of the brass blades. Pigeon jerked twice on the cable to signal Jake that his job was complete.

Jake secured the other end of the cable to the two-inch line leading to the trawler's anchor—fifteen feet below and fast in the muddy bottom of the bay. He then let his end of the cable slide down the rope and under the surface. The cable now hung beneath the *Miss Anh* from anchor line to propeller.

Moments later, Pigeon popped up on the far side of the skiff with a loud gasp for air. His wet blond hair draped over his face. Breathless, he grabbed the rail with both hands.

"Dammit, git in," Jake whispered as he scrambled to help Pigeon climb into the small boat. "Git in."

Pigeon put his foot on the lower end of an outboard motor and flipped over the stern, landing shoulder-first at the bottom of the boat. "Shit," he hissed, then squirmed onto the stern thwart.

Jake set the oars, spun the skiff, and pulled away from the trawler with jerking strokes. Darkness filled the quickly expanding space between trawler and skiff. When they were out of earshot, Pigeon fired up the outboard, handled the tiller, and motored toward the Point—toward the mainland shore where casino lights cast brilliant purple, green, and yellow streaks across the smooth water.

The skiff drew a V-shaped wake as it skimmed under the highway drawbridge and around Point Cadet. The brothers followed the channel markers, red and green, into Back Bay. They passed boatyards and dry docks filled with schooners, catboats, prams, and cabin cruisers; aging warehouses left dilapidated after long-forgotten storms; colorful shrimp boats tied up to docks with their outriggers pointing to the night sky; and shrimp packing plants with darkened windows and empty lots. On the Point, behind the wharves, plants, and boatyards was a tidy neighborhood of small clapboard houses arranged in blocks going north, south, east, and west. For three centuries, successive waves of immigrant fishermen and their families—the Spanish, the French, the Yugoslavs, and the Vietnamese—occupied this low-lying spit of land between the bays.

The brothers glided by bulkheads protecting the broad lawns of stately homes and private docks jutting out into the shallow water. Six-inch round Styrofoam balls, floating on the surface and painted in colorful patterns to claim the crab traps below, slipped by. Further up the channel, where Back Bay narrowed, a thick strip of salt grass abutted the dark pine forest at the water's edge, obscuring the transition from land to sea. Thin crosscut canals in the dull marsh, leading to shacks hidden in the woods, flashed with reflected light as the boat passed.

Hours before daybreak, before the release of the Coast's nighttime slumber and stillness, Pigeon ran the skiff through a narrow cut in the salt grass and onto the muddy bank of an old fishing camp their father used to rent.

On impact, Jake lurched forward in the boat. *It wasn't right,* he thought. Then he pulled a slight smile over his face as he reconciled with what was to become of the *Miss Anh* in just a few hours.

CHAPTER 2

Da Nang Air Base, Republic of Vietnam, December 13, 1970

Senior Airman Rex Thompson stepped out of a Quonset hut into the midday heat and humidity of Southeast Asia. An acrid smell of burnt jet fuel and a wet-dog stink of stagnant water hung heavy in the air. Rex walked a muddy path flanked by walls of dirty-white sandbags. The rumble of jet engines, the beat of helicopter rotors, and the echo of bombs beyond distant hills made it impossible to ignore the battle being choreographed around him.

Rex had an easy smile, many acquaintances, but few friends. On this, his second tour in Vietnam, he had just marked his twenty-third birthday. His first stint began after the Tet Offensive in 1968 at the Bien Hoa Air Base near Saigon and lasted for one year. This time the Air Force sent him to the 366th Tactical Fighter Wing at the Da Nang Air Base, one hundred and sixty kilometers south of the Demilitarized Zone and the North Vietnamese Army.

Rex entered a wooden building, ducking through the door into a small room his unit shared with the South Vietnamese airmen. A whiff of fermented *nuoc mam,* like rotting fish, hit Rex as soon as he entered. "Damn dinks," he said aloud to nobody but himself.

Burned-out bulbs and sticky yellow tape hung from a low ceiling. Except for scattered wooden tables, chairs, and a small kitchenette, the area was empty. Dirty pots and tin plates littered the countertops. Flies, not yet stuck to the yellow tape, buzzed. For Rex, sharing this dining room with Asians now touched a nerve. The feeling of excitement and bravado for fighting a war halfway around the globe for a country and a cause he did not understand had left him. He grabbed a Coke from the refrigerator and slipped out.

Back inside the Quonset hut, Rex knocked the mud off his boots, sipped his soda, and sat down at his desk to a stack of papers. A small tabletop fan spun hot air into his face. Surrounding him were a dozen steel tables with wooden chairs in two rows facing the door. All were empty. It was Sunday; the supply office should have been shut.

Another fighter jet took off with a growl to bomb the Ho Chi Minh Trail, the A Shaw Valley, Cambodia, or elsewhere. Rex didn't care. The building rattled and then quieted again to the buzz of his fan.

From his shirt pocket, Rex removed an airmail envelope and held it at arm's length. He had been carrying the letter around for the past week, unopened. The note was another from Deborah in Galveston, his once-girlfriend, who claimed he was the father of her newborn son. Rex drew the envelope to his nose. It lacked a scent of perfume, unlike the first several letters he received from her and had not answered. He tore the envelope in half, in quarters, then tossed the pieces into a galvanized can next to his desk.

Rex slumped in his chair and looked around the room. Two small windows flanked the front entrance. A separate door at the other end of the building led to a back office. The two featureless, corrugated steel sidewalls of the hut curved overhead to meet at the top. *I work upside-down in a got-damn pig trough,* he thought. A mortar round then popped somewhere up the river valley, far away. He shuddered, and his fingertips tingled. Ten months *up-country* near the DMZ, he felt his nerves unraveling.

He pulled a drawer entirely out of his desk and removed an envelope taped to the back. Within the fold were a key and a scrap of paper with a six-digit number. He spun the key between his thumb and forefinger for several minutes. Nobody had come to the supply office all morning, and he expected nobody would.

Rex rose from his chair, opened the back office door with the key, and flipped on the light. The room was empty except for a large wooden desk, three metal chairs, and a three-foot-square safe on the floor. He closed the door behind him, pulled up a seat, and spun the dial to the combination he had committed to memory. The steel door opened with a click.

Inside was a single shoebox containing stacks of crisp twenty-dollar bills. Purple paper bands held bundles of two thousand dollars each—twenty-three bundles, forty-six thousand dollars.

Rex paused to listen and heard nothing but the hum of his fan outside the door. He grabbed a nylon mail pouch off the floor and stuffed it with the cash. He zipped the bag, locked the safe, and wiped the dial and handle with his shirttail. The room was quiet. Rex turned to leave and noticed a framed photo of his master sergeant and family posing at some vacation lakefront on the desk. Mom, dad, sister, and little brother—the whole clan in swimsuits and life vests—all seemed to be looking right at him. Feeling a chill, Rex slipped the pouch under his arm and straightened his fatigues. He opened the office door and stepped into the main room.

Captain Nguyen Duc Dung halted halfway up the aisle between the desks when the door opened. He saw Rex emerge from a room in which he had no business.

"*Tròi oi* !" Captain Dung said.

The men paused, facing each other, only ten feet apart—Rex a head taller.

The South Vietnamese Army liaison officer stood with his head held high, shoulders pulled back, and arms akimbo. His presence in the supply office surprised Rex. Dung rarely came to this part of the base—and never on Sunday.

"What you doing?" Dung asked in English. Years of combat and military training in his war-torn country had fixed in him a profound sense of right and wrong. He suspected a wrong.

"Uh, just workin', sir," Rex shot back, trying to act calm.

"You lie, Thompson."

"Captain Dung, my unit got the day off, all but me." Rex omitted that he was currently on a punitive detail for insubordination.

"Nonsense."

"Just locking things up, sir," Rex said as he stepped toward the outside door.

Dung grabbed Rex's elbow with a firm grip when he tried to pass. "Sit down, airman."

Rex was a year or two younger than Captain Dung. He could have overpowered Dung and bolted through the door. *Play it cool*, he thought, and he sat. Dung had not yet discovered his crime.

Dung snatched the pouch from Rex's arms. "What's this?" He opened the zipper and emptied the cash on a nearby desk. Dung took a step back, unsnapped his leather holster, and palmed the handle of his sidearm. The whirl of the desk fan made the edges of the bills flutter. The beat of a nearby helicopter measured out time in short intervals, escalating the tension in the room. Both men knew the US government had sent this money to the South Vietnamese Army for their use. It was now evident to Captain Dung that he had intercepted a crime, and he was obliged to report Rex to the Air Force command; Rex would be court-martialed and sent home in chains.

They stared at each other for a long moment.

"Sir, I found the safe open," Rex said. "Someone left it unlocked. There was money—"

"Shut up."

"Captain, I didn't know who unlocked the safe. I was fixing to take the money over to headquarters where they'd keep it 'till tomorrow and . . ." Rex started to ramble before he realized he was digging a hole with his story. The room seemed to heat up, and sweat dripped down the back of his neck.

For the past few months, a strained relationship had festered between the South Vietnamese and the American military in Da Nang. Captain Dung's mind raced. He thought about the Vietnamese girl—young, only thirteen—raped by an American lieutenant. She was a colonel's daughter, well-connected. Watching the accused stand trial forced her family's pain deep into his mind. Dung didn't know the colonel or the girl. He didn't know the lieutenant either. But he knew the story, and the story clung to the base like wet air.

Dung recognized the dilemma he faced. If he accused this airman of thievery, another high-profile court-martial would broaden the discord between two countries who were trying to act as allies. Furthermore, marching a US serviceman at gunpoint on the base's American side could spark a misunderstanding, a fatal firefight. Perhaps there was an innocent explanation for why this airman was carrying the cash. He thought about what would be best for South Vietnam.

Dung moved forward, placing the money in the bag and shoving it in Rex's chest. "Put back in safe, now," Dung ordered. His temples were throbbing.

"It's locked. Don't know the combination,"

"*Bullsheet.*" Dung raised his Colt .45 M1911 semi-automatic pistol and aimed it at Rex's forehead. "Don't mess with me, airman."

Rex grabbed the pouch then hustled into the back office with a muzzle pushed between his shoulder blades. He sat in front of the safe and fumbled with the combination. Three times he failed to unlock the door.

Dung became impatient. He knew the longer this dragged out, the more likely there would be trouble. "Move," Dung said. He pushed Rex aside, spun the correct numbers on the dial, and opened the safe.

"You sure 'bout this?" Rex asked. "I was figgerin', split sixty-forty? Captain Dung, ain't nobody needs to know that—"

"No. Put in box." Dung cocked the hammer of his .45 with his thumb.

Rex stacked the bundles of twenties in the safe and laid the bag on the floor. Dung reached over and pushed the door closed, locking it with a twist of its handle.

"You go now," Dung commanded as he gripped his pistol with both hands. Rex scurried down the aisle between the desks and out the door. Standing alone in the Quonset, Dung wondered if he hadn't mistaken the airman's intentions. Perhaps the safe was left open, and the GI told the truth. Or, perhaps he was stealing. Dung holstered his weapon and hoped he had made the right decision.

• • •

Rex wandered about the air base to nowhere in particular. His head swam with what just happened. He found himself at the edge of the runway and sat on a pile of sandbags.

What the hell? Why did Dung let him off? Why didn't he lockstep him down to the SPs and have him arrested? He could have taken the cash for himself. Nothing made sense to him. Still, this wasn't Vietnamese money, he reasoned. It didn't belong in this country. He didn't belong in this goddamn country. The futility of the war was transparent to him now. *Two months and a wake-up*, he thought, and he was out of this shithole.

Rex looked east across the airfield, through the smoke and haze of the Han River Valley, and could see the blue-green hue of the Ba Na Hills, thirty kilometers away. Years ago, the colonial French built summer resorts in these highlands to escape the coastal lowlands' oppressive heat. Now, this area was crawling with Vietcong guerillas. Rex wondered if *Charlie* enjoyed the fresh mountain air today before sneaking down tonight to frag his ass with 140 mm Soviet-made rockets. In the past ten months, the enemy had fired dozens of missiles from dirt ramps in his direction. Eventually, he thought, his number would come up—dismembered, disemboweled, decapitated.

An F-4 Phantom jet screamed in low over Rex's head on its approach to the runway. He looked up and noticed the ordnance hardpoints under its wings were empty—the bombs it let loose cratered roads, blew villages apart, destroyed jungle canopy, and slaughtered warrior and civilian alike. In this war, it was hard to know the battle lines, hard to know the enemy. Rex cupped his palms around his mouth. "Fuck this fuckin' got-damn war!" he screamed back at the passing jet. Hot exhaust blasted him in the face, and he covered his eyes.

• • •

Hours later, after darkness descended on the air base, Rex Thompson fumbled with a flashlight hanging on a hook right inside the Quonset door.

The flashlight burned with a red glow, just enough light to see the double rows of desks and the open door at the far end of the room. Again, Rex sat on the floor in front of the safe and spun the dial. Inside, the eleven bundles of cash were as he had left them earlier in the day. Once more, Rex collected the bills into the mail pouch. He then ducked out of the hut, this time unchecked.

Airman Rex Thompson never saw Captain Nguyen Duc Dung in Vietnam again. Nobody ever questioned him about the safe or the money. Two months later, he shipped home to Texas with his pockets full of twenties. At that time, he thought he was forever leaving behind the people of the *Land of the Ascending Dragon*. But he was mistaken.

* * *

CHAPTER 3

Biloxi, August 17, 1993

A stiff breeze coming out of the south caused a light chop on the Biloxi Bay as the *Luce II* pushed through the railroad swing bridge and into the wind. A front was coming in, thought Blaise Baronich as he stood at the helm of his shrimper in the early morning hours. The weather today would not be suitable for fishing. The commercial shrimping season was just five months long in Mississippi, and he had already missed three weeks of it because of a broken winch. Other boats had a jump start on him, and he would play catch up all season long. This trip would last a week if he were catching shrimp, shorter if he burned his profit in diesel.

In the channel between Deer Island and Marsh Point, the open water and sky had the same faint monochromatic hue, rendering the horizon invisible. Blaise kept his eye on the water in front and scanned for bright channel markers mounted on pilings sunk into the shallow bottom of the bay. He didn't need his Loran to navigate these waters; he knew his location day and night. His concern was that another boat would cross his path, or its crew would be stupid enough to anchor in the channel before him. He checked his radar.

Blaise was a third-generation shrimper. His grandfather came from

Yugoslavia in the 1920s to fish and seek a dream. His grandfather named his first boat the *Luce* after his grandmother, whom everyone called Baba. Hurricane Camile destroyed the *Luce* in 1969, so Blaise's father had the *Luce II* built at the Stanovich Boatyard on Back Bay. She was an exceptional trawler and could take a bit of heavy weather. Blaise had worked the boat with his daddy since he was fourteen. For the past twenty years, he had taken its helm.

Blaise sensed the oil before he saw its subtle iridescent sheen on the water. The flattening of the wavelets caused by the slippery surface first caught his attention. Then came the sweet scent of gear oil, barely perceptible. His boat could smell like this, too, so he thrust his head out the pilothouse window to make sure the tang of oil was coming off the wind.

"Damn workboats," Blaise said to himself. He had seen it before many times, tugs and supply craft emptying their oil-laden bilges into the sound under cover of darkness. His livelihood and that of all the other shrimpers and oystermen on the Gulf depended on clean water. He could feel his head pound as his blood boiled. "Calm down," he told himself, trying to control his mounting anger.

The green glow of the radar screen then showed a signal return on the bow's starboard side, beyond the oil film. Blaise thought this was odd. The radar blip was faint and far outside the channel, unlikely to be the hull of a boat or marker. Blaise strained his eyes to look past the oil. He then spun the helm and guided the *Luce II* into shallow water.

"Jacko, come up here," Blaise yelled into the depth of his boat.

Jacko, his new deckhand, was shoveling some of the thirty-three shaved blocks of ice stored in the hold from one side to the other to trim the boat. This trip marked the start of his first shrimping season. Jacko climbed into the pilothouse, where Blaise scanned the water with binoculars.

"What's up, Cap?" Jacko asked with a bit of excitement.

"Look there," Blaise said, pointing a finger to a section of water framed by a silhouette of pine trees on Deer Island.

Jacko took the glasses and saw the rigging of a shrimp boat rising from the water like a cluster of broken reeds. The vessel listed to the starboard side as if it were resting on the shallow bottom. The port outrigger pointed straight up with a shroud of black nets hanging from the top. Jacko could make out the shape of a man standing on the slanting roof of a green pilothouse, barely visible above the water's surface. The man was frantically waving his arms.

Blaise pushed the throttle forward, and the *Luce II* got up to a hull speed of ten knots. As they closed in on the trawler, he ordered Jacko to elevate their outriggers and secure their tackle. As the *Luce II* came up alongside the wreckage, Blaise thought he recognized the boat as the *Chasin' Tail*, known around the harbor as the *Christmas Yacht*. He saw the man standing on the pilothouse was barefoot, wet, and wore nothing but a white undershirt and a pair of khaki shorts.

The *Luce II* backed up to the port side of the submerged boat. The man dove into the water and swam to a ladder Jacko had dropped over the side.

"Don, Mr. Don. He's still down there," the young man said as he struggled up the ladder. His eyes flashed with intensity.

"Who's that?" Jacko asked, grabbing the man by the arms and hauling him over the rail.

"Mr. Don. He didn't come up."

"What?"

"He's in the boat," the man said.

"Drowned! No shit," Jacko said. "Ya think he's dead?"

Blaise emerged from the pilothouse with a blanket for the young man. "Who's dead?"

"Mr. Nguyen," the man said. "He, he didn't get out."

"Who?"

"Don Nguyen."

"How long ago?"

"Hours."

"Where?" Blaise asked.

"Engine room, I think."

Jacko said, "Never came up? Man, that's brutal."

"I dove for him over and over, couldn't find him."

"What's the boat?" Blaise asked.

"*Miss Anh.*"

"You?"

"Timmy Truong."

"Anyone else on board?"

"No, just Mr. Don and me," Timmy said and then glanced at the deck, looking for a place to sit.

"Shit, think he's dead?" Jacko asked.

"Jacko, take Timmy to the galley and get him dried up," Blaise said before stepping back into the pilothouse.

Blaise knew Don Nguyen. Don was not only a hard-working shrimper but a successful businessman. He owned four other boats at the harbor and always found good captains and crew to work for him. *Damn, he just drowned.* Blaise remembered the wooden-hulled trawler, the *Chasin' Tail,* built somewhere over near Galveston, was repossessed by the bank. In some fashion, Don must have recently acquired the boat and renamed it.

The *Luce II* pulled thirty yards away from the *Miss Anh.* Blaise dropped anchor and called the Coast Guard on the VHF radio.

"I know this dude," Jacko said, climbing up into the pilothouse to talk to Blaise. "Went to Magnolia together."

"How's he doing?" Blaise asked.

"Warming up, still shaking like a leaf. I think his nerves are shot. Man, this shit's bunk."

"Did you get him something to eat?"

"He just got hitched to Anh Nguyen, Mr. Don's girl. I guess it's Truong now," Jacko said. "Yeah, coffee and one of those cheddar biscuits." Jacko sat on a bench and stared out the window. "Mr. Don just scored that boat for Timmy and Anh. Think as a wedding gift or somepin. Was going to make Timmy a shrimper."

"You don't want to sit with him until the Coast Guard comes?"

"No, Cap. I'm just a little whacked right now."

"How so?"

"Ya know, Mr. Don cashed out with the boat down there, and all."

"Okay, watch for the Coasties," Blaise said before dropping down the ladder to the galley.

• • •

The following day, the *Coast Sentinel* newspaper had a front-page article with a full-color photo of the green pilothouse roof and rigging just above the water's surface. Floating orange booms, stained with brown oil, surrounded the wreckage. Captured in the background was the marshy coastline of a barrier island hosting a copse of storm-battered pines. The lead story told how the *Miss Anh* had sunk in fourteen feet of water and how authorities recovered Don Nguyen's body from the engine room. The piece continued:

> A passing boat rescued Timmy Truong several hours after the sinking, and paramedics took him to a local hospital for evaluation. An investigation is underway to find the cause of the wreckage and drowning. However, divers said a hole had been ripped through the boat's bottom and into the engine room. Mr. Nguyen may have been trapped by flooding water and perished below decks.
>
> At the hospital, Mr. Truong told police that when he started the engine to move the boat off its anchor, he felt a jolt and heard a loud noise in the vessel. The trawler sank so fast Mr. Truong did not have time to send out a distress signal. He dove several times for Mr. Nguyen, the boat owner, but could not find him.

• • •

Jake finished reading the article for the second time, then went outside the camp to vomit. *Both of them should have been able to get off the goddamn boat*, he thought. What the hell was Nguyen doing in the engine room, anyways, that time of the morning? This was not the way it was supposed to happen.

Jake was still shaken and feeling ill, twenty-four hours after he first heard there was a death on the *Miss Anh*. Reading the newspaper intensified his anxiety. It was one thing to scuttle a boat; a drowning was quite another. Now that the stakes were jacked up to murder, he and Pigeon needed to work out a better plan to disguise their motives, strengthen their alibis. Jake looked off into the nearby woods, running his mind with what he should do next.

Pigeon stepped through the doorframe and held the screen open with his sore shoulder. A purpling bruise emerged from the edge of his cotton shirt, where the sleeves were torn off. "Those got-damn chinks got what's coming," he said with a lit Marlboro dangling from his lower lip. "Can't just yank another man's property without expect—"

"Shut your face," Jake said.

"Don't shit me like that, bro. You know that boat didn't rightly belong to 'em."

"You don't git it, do you?" Jake asked while trying to fight off his nausea.

"Nguyen had it coming, man," Pigeon said, then pulled deep on his cigarette and blew white smoke in Jake's direction.

With both hands on his knees, Jake stooped forward to retch. His shoulder-length brown hair fell over his face. After three dry heaves, he looked up at his younger brother. "This fucks everything," he said. "Keep your got-damn trap shut, or you'll be spending the rest of your shit life in Parchman."

"Would you chill out, man? Would ya? I ain't saying shit."

Jake worried. He knew Pigeon all too well. He was spontaneous, impulsive, and a braggart, much like their father. It would be hard for him to keep quiet about the boat. He'd get doped up with his friends and let slip the tiniest of details—particulars connecting them to the murder. Jake held his dark hair back with his hand and heaved again.

CHAPTER 4

1st Division Army Headquarters, Hue, South Vietnam, March 15, 1971

Captain Dung stood ramrod straight in the center of a room with wrists pushed to his hips and fingers flexed into his sweaty palms. Sharp creases pressed in his khaki uniform emphasized his respect for his station. He looked straight-ahead to a small blue banner, bordered in white with a single Arabic numeral "1," hanging from a nail behind a large wooden desk. Dung dared not divert his eyes. He unlocked his knees and crimped his toes to keep blood flowing to his feet. Sunlight streamed into the room through large windows overlooking the inner walls of Hue's ancient citadel, one hundred kilometers north of Da Nang.

The man seated behind the desk before him, General Ngo Van Cu, commander of the 1st Army Division, required no introduction. General Cu wore a brown-green cap perched high on his big head, the visor embroidered with heavy bullion. An oversized spread-eagle gold badge tipped the front rim even higher. Shadows in deep acne scars darkened his face.

Standing at Dung's side, Colonel Le Dinh Lao addressed the general in Vietnamese, "Sir, a commission has charged Captain Dung with failure to safeguard the valuable assets of the armed forces of the Republic of Vietnam."

Colonel Lao was two inches shorter than Dung. The colonel stood erect with his chest full of ribbons pushed out. From his left shoulder, braided cords hung over a bright blue 1st Division patch. He wore a painter's brush mustache and a red beret over his tiny head in the flamboyant style of South Vietnam's vice president, Nguyen Cao Ky.

"On December 13th, during his usual duties as a liaison officer to the United States Air Force 366th Fighter Wing in Da Nang, Captain Dung intercepted a United States Air Force senior airman committing a crime. Captain Dung failed to take appropriate action, which resulted in the loss of forty-six thousand US dollars from the Republic of Vietnam."

Not that simple, Dung thought, as he listened to the allegations against him.

Colonel Lao continued, "We convened an appropriate commission to investigate Captain Dung's conduct and found him irrefragably culpable."

There was no commission, no inquiry, no trial, and no justice, Dung knew. He had tried to explain his rationale for not arresting Airman Thompson, but his superiors failed to listen. He told them that Thompson had provided a plausible story of an open safe and the need to protect the cash. Dung related his hesitation in marching Thompson across the base and the misinterpretation it might generate. He had reported his encounter with Airman Thompson to Colonel Lao that same day. The next day, Colonel Lao arrested him when he found the money missing.

"Captain Dung has brought great shame to his unit and all the brave and honorable soldiers of the Republic of Vietnam."

I didn't steal the cash, Dung wanted to scream in his defense. Dung had told his commanders he suspected Thompson returned that same night and reopened the safe. But as he learned, nobody ever questioned Thompson or looked for the money.

"This officer has been relieved of his duties as the army liaison at Da Nang Air Base. He is, therefore, available for reassignment. I recommend that he be transferred at once to the 1st Armored Brigade under the command of Colonel Nguyen Trong Luat."

The colonel was sending him on a suicide mission, Dung realized. As Lao spoke, the 1st Armored Brigade was fighting its way out of Laos and back to South Vietnam. The unit was part of Operation Lam Son 719, a failed offensive incursion into Laos to disrupt the North Vietnamese Army's supply lines. Six weeks earlier, the Army of the Republic of Vietnam, with US forces' help, had beat their way west on Route 9, past Khe Sanh, to the Laotian border. From there, the South Vietnamese 1st and 2nd Divisions had pushed into Laos. The South, however, had met fierce resistance from the North and sustained massive casualties.

The 1st Corps commander General Hoang Xuan Lam and President Nguyen Van Thieu now ordered all South Vietnamese forces from Laos. Dung recognized that only a well-disciplined and organized military could execute an orderly retreat from battle. The Army of the Republic of Vietnam did not own these qualities.

The communist forces had surrounded the 1st Armored Brigade and were assaulting the fleeing column at every chance as it headed to the border along the clogged and congested Route 9. Dozens of destroyed tanks and armored personnel carriers cluttered the narrow road. Dung knew the retreat would soon turn into a rout.

"Sir, as you are aware, the 1st Armored Brigade has fought with courage toward their objective in Tchepone. Unfortunately, they have experienced significant casualties from NVA artillery and require an additional company commander as they move through the Se Pone River Valley. Captain Dung can join the brigade by chopper as soon as tonight if this is what you wish."

General Cu, who had not uttered a word in Dung's presence, nodded his head.

"Yes, sir," Colonel Lao responded.

Two military policemen wearing tan-brown camouflage escorted Captain Dung out of the headquarters building and to a debris-strewn field in the citadel's Mang Ca sector. Dung climbed into the back seat of a waiting jeep and rode past bombed-out palaces and shrines and the crumbling walls of the ancient fortress. The vehicle stopped at the remnants of the Hien Ngon Gate on the eastern side of the inner city. Dung got out and paused for a moment in front of the center of three blue arches. A beady-eyed dragon with large white teeth and a flaming mane glared at him from the top of the archway. Twenty meters further up, more dragons and flames decorated three smaller arches and the partially collapsed tile roofline. A colorful palette of red, blue, green, and yellow adorned an elaborate frieze surrounding the edifice.

Pushed through the gateway with the broadside of a baton, Dung entered the Forbidden Purple City grounds. Once the sanctuary of emperors, concubines, and eunuchs, the palace—built by the Nguyen Dynasty—now lay in ruin. North Vietnamese and American bombing of Hue during the Tet Offensive had destroyed the city. Rubble littered the once-grand plazas and boulevards. For a moment, Dung regretted never visiting this magnificent fortress in its previous state of grandeur.

A Huey *slick* with US Army markings sat in the middle of a vast courtyard with its rotor in a slow spin. The guards shepherded Dung onto the waiting helicopter and strapped him to a jump seat. As the rotor picked up speed, Dung reached into his pocket and removed a letter he had penned the night before to his wife in Quang Ngai. He scribbled GONE TO LAOS on the back of the addressed envelope with a pencil and handed it to the military policeman standing right outside the open aircraft door. The man held the letter for a moment before it fell through his fingers to the ground. Quickly, he trapped the envelope with the toe of his boot as the helicopter kicked up dust. Then staring at Captain Dung, he ground the note into the dirt.

CHAPTER 5

The Gulf of Mexico, off the Texas coast, April 30, 1975

At sunrise, an aluminum crew boat plied the crystal Gulf water, forty miles south of Galveston Island. Gentle swells broadsided the craft and rolled it from side to side. Rex Thompson sat in a molded fiberglass seat where he could see out a window. He kept his gaze on the horizon to calm his queasy stomach. The boat was carrying him home from a thirty-day stint on an oil rig off the coast of Texas. His job as a roughneck had two significant benefits: the pay was decent, and the work got him out of the house for a month at a time.

Rex thought about how Deborah would greet him when he got home. She would pepper him with weeks' worth of complaints and problems: a stopped-up sink, a fallen fence, or trouble in the neighborhood with the boys.

From his wallet, he removed a wrinkled black-and-white snapshot of Deborah and him on their wedding day. The photo was taken four years earlier, just weeks after his Air Force discharge. In the picture, he had a dark three-week beard, and his hair was still military-short. He remembered Deborah insisting he wear a collared shirt for the occasion. The grainy image showed her swollen breasts in the plunging neckline of a revealing white dress. She held their baby, Jake, in her arms.

Through the glass window, wet with salt spray, Galveston's skyline appeared on the northern horizon.

Rex thought about when he first met his son, bounced him on his knee like a cockhorse, and reveled in his cooing and gurgling. It was then he first gave serious thought to a life with Deborah. A preacher who lived near her folks' house married them a week later. They had their first argument as husband and wife on their wedding night. Deborah was hot-tempered, passionate, and intense; their sex was the same. Soon, they had another son whom they called Peter.

The crew boat tied up at Galveston Wharves. Two dozen men filed off the gangplank without a sense of urgency. Rex grabbed a duffle of dirty clothes, stood on the dock, and scanned the parking lot for Deborah and his truck. When she failed to show as the lot emptied out, he decided to stop in at Sisters Bar—a choice he had made many times in the past—for a beer or two before catching a cab home. A little buzz in the morning, he thought, would help him get through the rest of the day.

At a street corner one block from the bar, a headline in a newspaper rack caught his attention, SURRENDER! SAIGON YIELDS TO REDS. Rex put a quarter into the slot, pulled open the window, and removed a copy. After more than two decades of war between North and South Vietnam, the battle was over. Photographs of South Vietnamese families struggling to leave the country, as General Giap's communist forces surrounded Saigon, filled the newspaper's front page. There were images of civilian mobs storming the American Embassy's gates and thousands of former soldiers clamoring aboard ships, barges, boats, and anything that floated in the Saigon Harbor. Rex opened the paper to read about the fifty-eight thousand Americans, two hundred and fifty thousand South Vietnamese soldiers, and an estimated one million civilians who lost their lives in the futile war. *For what?*

The paper told of President Thieu's escape to Taiwan and the US ambassador's helicopter rescue from the embassy's roof. American ships off the coast collected tens of thousands of panicked refugees who arrived in all manner of boats and aircraft. Reports predicted that the hundreds of thousands of South Vietnamese left behind, those who had fought for their country or worked for the Americans, would soon find themselves crushed by the brutal communist dictatorship of Le Duan. The speed at which the country collapsed in the past four weeks while Rex was working offshore surprised him. Bitterness toward his government, the war, the Vietnamese—North and South—and his *wasted* years rose like bile in his throat. Rex tossed the newspaper into a trash can and pulled on the door to Sisters Bar.

• • •

"Hey, Daddy." Four-year-old Jake greeted Rex with a hug at the front door of his house.

"How's my little buddy?" Rex asked. He threw down his bag, grabbed Jake, and tossed him in the air. Jake had the same pale skin and dark hair as himself. "Where's your little brother?"

"Backyard with Momma." Jake giggled. Rex put him down, and Jake tore through the house and out the back door.

Rex walked through his small two-bedroom home, stepping over children's toys and dirty laundry. He glanced in the kitchen to see dishes stacked in the sink. A cat he did not recognize hissed at him from behind an open bedroom door. He walked into the family room, paneled in dark wood. The den was furnished with a tan sectional sofa, a brass-and-glass coffee table smeared with handprints and food, and a braided blue rug. A pile of dirty sheets filled a corner.

"Who the hell lives like this?" Rex hollered through the open screen door. Nobody responded. Rex stepped onto the small wooden landing to see Deborah in a faded pink housecoat, reclining in a beach chair by a tiny plastic pool in the backyard. She had a cigarette in one hand and a tumbler in the other. Peter, in underpants, sat in the water at her feet. Rex stumbled down the back steps.

"You're goddamn drunk," Deborah said, not getting up. "Jesus, for the boys' sake, can't you come home sober?"

Rex ignored his wife and looked at three-year-old Peter. How small and frail his son appeared. He had his mother's blond hair, but nothing else reminded him of her. Peter had a narrow face that made his sharp nose stick out. The neighborhood kids teased, saying that he looked like a little bird, and took to calling him *Pigeon*, a nickname that stuck.

Rex sidestepped Deborah and reached for Peter in the pool. "Come here, little man," Rex said. He picked the boy up and placed him on his shoulders. Jake came running over. Rex took off around the backyard with one son holding on to his head while the other gave chase.

Deborah took a drag from her cigarette then flicked the butt into the pool water. As Rex ran past, she looked at him with disdain. "Washer's broke," she said, then got up from her chair, went into the house, and turned on the TV.

• • •

The following morning, Rex returned to Sisters Bar. The room was dark, lit only by a dim light over the backbar and a green neon sign advertising Jack Daniels above a dartboard. Ellis and Keith were perched, as usual, on stools near the entrance. They nodded to Rex when he entered, then turned back to nurse their beers.

Sherie stood behind the bar, wiping water spots off the glassware and tidying up the place after the previous night that was rougher than usual. Rex liked to come in when Sherie was working. She had an easy way of making him feel welcome with small talk and an occasional seductive smile. She had a figure needing nothing more than a pair of tight jeans and a low-cut halter top, showing her generous cleavage, to get most men's attention.

"What you having, Rex?" Sherie asked. She leaned in toward him with both hands on the countertop and let the soft curls of her long, dark hair cascade forward over her chest, tempting Rex to divert his eyes from hers.

"Shiner, Sherie," Rex said with a subtle grin. He pulled up a stool at the far side of the bar from Ellis and Keith. Rex thought one of these days for fun, he would say *Sherry*, Sherie, even though he drank nothing but bourbon and beer—Shiner Bock when he could get it. The barroom was cold, quiet, and had the familiar scent of peanuts, rye, hops, and tobacco. Rex glanced around the room. Billiard balls sat racked up on green felt. Black Formica tables, with chairs still turned upside down on their tops, stood scattered about the floor. *Another day*.

Rex looked down the length of the bar to where Ellis and Keith leaned over their brews. Both men wore extra-large faded jean shorts, which enveloped the stools on which they were sitting. Tight T-shirts with washed-out fishing logos struggled to contain their generous guts. Strands of thin gray hair fell from their balding heads.

Sherie slid the pale draft across the bar with a napkin to follow. The lager soothed Rex's throat, which was sore from a night of yelling at his wife. He needed a change.

"Sherie," Rex called her in close and directed her gaze to Keith and Ellis. He whispered in her ear, "Get 'em some red ball caps, and they two could pass as Tweedledee and 'Dum."

She smiled, studied the two regulars for a minute, then returned to the center of the bar, where she bent over to unpack a case of liquor on the floor. All three men watched.

Ellis then turned to Rex and called out, "You want to buy a boat?"

"What's that?"

"A boat, Rex. You hankering for a boat?"

"Sure, man," Rex shot back, not thinking Ellis was serious.

"A guy I know has a forty-two-foot shrimper down at the dock. Fixing to unload it cheap. Will even float you a loan," Ellis said. "You can be your own boss. Shrimps are plenty out there."

From his stool, Keith nodded in agreement.

Rex knew next to nothing about shrimping. He was a fool to even consider buying a boat. Still, he thought, what harm could come from a look?

The boat was within walking distance of Sisters Bar. Rex, Ellis, and Keith ordered another round of beer in plastic cups, telling Sherie they would return soon. They headed out the back door to the dock.

The trawler was larger than Rex had envisioned. With her bow facing out, she rested in a slip on her mooring lines. From sturdy mounts, thirty-foot steel outriggers stood straight up on each side of the boat. Cable and lines hung in all directions from the top rigging. The hull was bright red and the pilothouse green. The name *Chasin' Tail* tagged the transom in large white letters. Brown rust bled down the freeboard.

A paper cup and an old red baseball cap floated on a seagrass mat surrounding the boat. Oily water rose and fell against the wooden planks of its hull. Rex noticed a hand-lettered cardboard sign tied to the boom, BOAT FOR SALE, FRESH SHRIMP. A stench of ripe seafood wafted in the air.

The three men stepped onto the aft part of the vacant boat. Dirty white buckets and a battered green Coleman ice chest littered the slick wooden deck. Rex studied the shiny brass drum of the main winch mounted behind the pilothouse.

"If you're a careless shit, that thing'll take your hand off, like that," Ellis said, snapping his fingers.

Rex looked up.

Keith added, "Yeah, years ago, my daddy chopped off some fingers in a winch like that. Never could tie laces again. Momma had to sew Velcro on his church shoes. Otherwise, he just wore rubber boots."

With a deadpan expression, Ellis added, "Heard your daddy use' tell down at the packing house that he lost his fingers in a *wench*."

"A wench?" Keith asked, not getting the pun.

"Yeah, in a wench. A girl." Ellis snickered. "Lost his fingers in a wench." With two fingers, he poked Keith in the arm.

"Ain't gittin my hand caught in that thing," Rex said, again looking at the winch drum. "Man, thought you guys were trying to git me to buy this tub?"

"We was. I like the name *Chasin' Tail*, don't you?" Ellis asked. "Makes you kind of feel free."

Rex nodded, then wandered up to the pilothouse and found the door unlocked. He stepped in and stood at the helm. Through several windows tilted out in front, he had a commanding view of the harbor.

Ellis poked his head in. "Looks good on you, man."

"You ever bust ass on a trawler before?" Rex asked.

"No, not me."

"I think I could."

"It's a hard life. Take you away from Deb and the boys a lot," Ellis said.

"Hell, I'm shipped out now for weeks at a time. If I git this, I'll be able to make my own way. Do it in my sweet time. Go out when I want, ya know. Catch my drift?"

"You should do it," Ellis said, and after a pause, "Hey, how're things with you and Deb anyways?"

"Not too good, man."

"Saw her and the boys at the grocer last week. She's a fine gal, Rex. Known her folks all my life. Good people."

"I know. Probably me. I'm looking for something," Rex said.

"Like what?"

"Don't know. Should've never tied down."

"What you talking like that for? You did it for Jake—that's good. What with a fox like Deb, you were bound to have more young'uns," Ellis said.

"I'm shit for a father. Debbie don't care squat for me."

"You can pull it together. I know it."

"Ellis, I have no freaking idea what I'm supposed to do as a father *or* a husband."

"You're a good father when you're home."

"You know, I never really knew my dad. Jeez, what I know ain't good," Rex said. "I'm afraid I'll turn out like him."

"That's crap. It don't work like that."

"Think it does, man."

Ellis paused and glanced around the pilothouse at various instruments mounted above the windows.

"Maybe a hardcore flip like this boat might help," Rex said. "It can't git much worse."

"Might set you straight, Rex, sure. Hey, I shouldn't be asking, but if you reckon to git this boat, where you fixin' to get the cash?"

"I got some dough put down."

"Like?"

"Let's just say, a little sweet Vietnamese severance package, 'nough for front money."

"Man, you're done set. Do it."

"Debbie don't know crap about the cash. Zip shit, okay?" Rex said.

Ellis pulled his thumb and fingertips across his pinched lips.

Both men walked back to the large working deck. Keith was down on hands and knees with his butt in the air, his head poked into an open hatch.

Ellis said to Rex, "That's where you keep your catch, down there on a heap of ice."

"Can you see the engine?" Rex asked Keith.

"Nope."

"Under that other hatch," Ellis said, pointing to a cover at the side of the deck. "You oughta go take a look. Here, gimme your beer."

Rex lifted a small hatch cover and peered down into a black hole to where a ladder descended. He eased himself into the compartment. It was dark, moist, and smelled of oil and mildew. Rex let his eyes adjust to the blackness while he tried to overcome a tinge of claustrophobia. After a moment, he could make out a massive Detroit Diesel, bolted to the wooden hull. A steel driveshaft ran aft to connect to the propeller. Rex knew nothing about maintaining a marine engine. He would learn, he told himself.

Rex climbed out of the engine room and closed the hatch. The boat seemed in good shape and only needed a little cleanup and paint. And hell, the stench suggested the vessel worked and could catch shrimp.

"Look here, Rex," Ellis said, taking a sip of Rex's beer and holding on to a vertical steel tower at midship. "You lower these outriggers and drop your nets into the water while you drive forward. These boards go up front the trawls and pulls 'em open in the water." Ellis kicked a sizeable wooden panel lashed to the inside rail. "Called doors."

Ellis then walked over to a light galvanized chain hanging with a net. He continued. "This's a 'tickler chain.' It drags on the sand in front of the trawls and kicks the lazy damn shrimp into the net. I'd call it a 'kick-ass chain' if it was me."

"How'd ya git so damn smart?" Rex asked in a sarcastic tone.

"Slept once with a girl whose daddy was a shrimper," Ellis said as he tossed Rex's empty beer cup into the water.

"Bullshit," Keith said. "You ain't never had no shrimper's daughter."

"Sure did. Had to let her go 'cuz all her kin stunk like stinking shrimp."

"Stinking shrimp," Rex said. "Man, that smells like money to me."

CHAPTER 6

Biloxi, January 1, 1983

He opened his eyes and gazed from the bed to the ceiling, where huge chunks of plaster were missing. Thin asbestos insulation hung between exposed batten boards. His room was bright, lit from a low winter's sun, streaming in through a third-story window of the Tivoli Hotel. The building faced the Biloxi Channel, Deer Island, and the Mississippi Sound. His head throbbed. His thick tongue stuck to the roof of his parched mouth. The sun was due south; *it must be about noon*, he thought. "God, I gotta clean my shit up this year," Rex Thompson mumbled. He'd made then broken many New Year's Day resolutions like this before.

Rex rolled to his side and saw that the girl was gone. *Desiré, Desire*—what the hell, he couldn't remember. He reached over to a nightstand and felt for his wallet. A lonely ten remained in the fold. The thought that she left him anything amused him. Rex pulled out a pair of plastic eyeglasses from under the covers with 1983 written across the front in silver glitter. He looked at the glasses, not remembering from where they came. Rex's mind was in a fog; he was having a tough time reconstructing the events of the night before. He put the glasses on his face as if they would offer a focus.

Except for hanging out at Arnie's Tavern to get an early start on New Year's Eve, meeting two young ladies who kept running their fingers through his short salt-and-pepper hair, and bringing one of them back to his room, the night was a blur. A new course, that's what he needed. Set a new course, he promised again.

Rex still had the *Chasin' Tail,* but not much else from the life he had started in Galveston twelve years earlier. He and Deborah had found it too hard to hold their marriage together and called it quits a few years back. Rex emersed himself in shrimping and enjoyed being his own boss. During the season, he could make the most money chasing the harvest for months from Corpus Christi to Apalachicola. Six months ago, he moved his boat to Biloxi and leased a berth on Back Bay. He was done with Galveston, done with Deborah. His move, however, made him miss his two boys even more. Despite promising to do so, he had never allowed himself to be a big part of their lives. Another resolution shattered.

Rex stepped out the back door of the hotel and headed north to Howard Avenue. He needed to check up on his boat, which was up on blocks for repairs to the hull. The sky was bright blue and accented with stiff white clouds. Through leafless cypress trees in their wintertime baldness, sharp rays of sunshine cast long shadows onto the street's gray asphalt. Like today, the clarity of the sky and sun only happened in Biloxi during the winter when frigid air pushed the haze of oppressive humidity out to sea. He knew it wouldn't stay fresh for long and that tropical weather would soon return with the first pink azalea blooms of mid-March.

He passed a commercial tackle supply where he had left three nets for mending. A Vietnamese family had recently bought the shop, and he hoped they would be around over the holiday. It wasn't their New Year's Day, after all. He remembered Tet was sometime later in January or February when they danced around in pajamas with a dragon puppet on their heads.

But the shop was closed for the American holiday as well. "Fuck it." So, they get to celebrate both new year's days. His bitterness toward the time he spent in Southeast Asia over a decade ago had never entirely left him. It pissed Rex off that reminders of the war were on the streets of

Biloxi, in his face. It seemed to him that everywhere on the Gulf Coast—Galveston included—the Vietnamese were taking over the fishing industry. They were buying up boats, ice houses, and tackle shops. It just wasn't right, he thought.

Rex turned up Oak Street and down Fifth Street as he walked to the boatyard. The *Chasin' Tail* rested in the yard on its sturdy wooden keel. Several jackscrews propped the hull in balance. Shipwrights had already started to replace a few planks near the waterline and scrape and sand the underside for a new coat of copper paint. Boatyards around the country weren't making wooden-hulled trawlers anymore and finding good tradesmen to work on them was a challenge. However, this craft was preserved in Biloxi—one reason Rex had made the Mississippi Coast his new home.

The sun threw sharp shadows between the dozen-or-so colorfully painted boats in the yard. The brilliant light made it difficult for Rex to open his eyes and triggered a screaming headache. "Nothing doing today," Rex said to himself. He put his palm up against the hull of his boat to check the seams. It would take several more weeks to complete the work on the *Chasin' Tail*. He was in no hurry; the shrimp season would not start for months.

As he turned to leave and go back to the Tivoli Hotel to lie down—or maybe to stop in at another dark lounge for what he really wanted, a stiff drink—he noticed, standing before him in the shade of his boat, a silhouette of a man he could never forget. Rex could not see the man's face, but his memory completed the details. Nguyen Duc Dung, for sure. It had been over twelve years since their brief encounter in Da Nang. He had often thought about how close he came to spending decades locked up at Fort Leavenworth. Smoldering in his mind was how Captain Dung put a gun to his head, then let him go. Rex immediately recognized Dung. Would Dung remember him?

• • •

Thuy Linh entered the sitting room through a beaded curtain, carrying a red lacquered tray with a teapot and two white cups. Her long black hair fell over the shoulder of her golden-yellow silk blouse as she placed the tray on a low table in front of her husband. She lifted her eyes from the tray and smiled at Dung.

Dung did not look up from where he sat cross-legged on a cushion. In Vietnamese, he said, "I saw the bastard from Da Nang this morning."

"*Anh ơi*, who are you talking about?" Linh asked.

"The guy who took the money."

"The money? You saw him here? In Biloxi?" Linh asked as she knelt at the table and poured green tea.

"The boatyard."

"Are you sure?"

"Of course, I am." Dung lifted the ceramic cup to his mouth and blew steam off the top. "How could I forget him? Do you know who I'm talking about? That man ruined my life."

Linh nodded and glanced around the room in the tiny house they rented on Point Cadet, near the docks and the shrimp-packing plants. It had been eight years since she, Dung, and their young daughter had been forced to leave their homeland at the end of the war.

"He looked at me, but I'm not sure he knew me," Dung said. His thick, calloused hands cupped the warm tea. Years of shucking oysters and picking shrimp had left his fingertips rough and scarred. "I was standing in the shadows when he glanced my way; then he turned and left."

"You must forget him. The war is done."

"But you know what he did to me?"

"I know. You forgive him and move on," Linh said.

Eleven-year-old Anh burst through the doorway with headphones on. "Mom, Dad, look what Jill got for Christmas last week," Anh said in English. "She let me borrow it this afternoon. So cool." She held out a bright pink cassette player for her parents to see.

Anh danced around the room in dark blue jeans and a matching denim jacket to music only she could hear. Her long black hair, like her mother's, swung from side to side in a ponytail. Thi Anh was just old enough to want to make her own decisions about her clothes and music. Watching Anh do an American twist moved Linh to think about her daughter's drift to the culture of their adopted home. Growing up would not be the same for Anh as it had been for her when she came of age in Vietnam.

"*Con* Thi Anh, run along. I'm talking to your father right now," Linh said in Vietnamese. She turned back to Dung. "I understand you feel anger toward that man, but you must let go."

Dung said nothing as Anh skipped into the kitchen. Then he finished his tea and placed the cup back on the tray. "I'm going back down to the docks to check on something." He pushed up and left the room.

Linh, still kneeling at the low table, did not look up or respond. They had left behind many awful memories of the war when they escaped to the sea and sought refuge in America. She now realized that even after many years, dark and painful thoughts of the war still burned in her husband's mind.

• • •

"Nancy, ever heard of a guy called Nguyen Dung?" Rex asked as Nancy refilled his mug with rich coffee.

"Yeah," Nancy said before turning to other customers in her tidy café just off the Vieux Marché. Nancy then moved about the bright room picking up dishes, pouring coffee, and making small talk with her regulars—small-town businessmen, bankers, shop owners, and fishermen.

Rex shook more salt on his plate of eggs and opened another packet of jelly for his grits. He looked across the room, studying the trophies and ribbons that had accumulated over the years on a shelf. The awards were from youth teams Nancy's Café had sponsored. A plaque on the most significant trophy read MISSISSIPPI SOUTHERN DISTRICT CHAMPIONS, LITTLE LEAGUE BASEBALL, 1979. Propped against the plinth was a faded photograph of a dozen boys with NANCY'S NUGGETS printed on their red jerseys. Rex thought of his own two sons, who still lived with their mother in Galveston.

"Goes now by Don Nguyen. Nobody calls him Dung these days," Nancy said. She pulled up a chair next to Rex to get off her feet for a moment and leaned in. "Why'd you ask?"

"Nothing," Rex said.

"But you asked. You just don't come in here asking for no reason. You know Don?"

"No. Can't say I do."

"Okay, Rex, you want anything else?" Nancy asked, motioning to the dirty plates in front of him.

"No, ma'am."

Nancy stood and wiped her hands with her apron. She picked up Rex's plates, cleaned the table, and slipped behind the counter. She had other customers to serve.

Rex looked up at the photograph again. The framed image reminded him of how much he had screwed up his life. He hadn't seen his boys in over a year. Jake was a good pitcher, he had heard, but he had never seen him play. Things could have been different if he had only tried harder, he thought.

"You have any kids?" Rex asked Nancy, who was across the room.

"No. You?"

"Two sons. They live with their mamma in Texas. Don't see 'em much."

"You should. What age?" Nancy walked over to Rex, sensing the conversation would become personal.

"Jake's twelve, and Pigeon just turned eleven."

"Pigeon?"

"Peter, but he goes by Pigeon."

"They need you now, Rex."

"Yeah." Rex stirred sugar into his coffee. "It's complicated. My fault. They have a fine mother."

"Rex, it's a new year. Call 'em."

"I got to do some figgerin' first." Rex looked up at Nancy. He saw she had tied her dark-brown hair into a tight bun on the back of her head and wore only a hint of makeup on her long, plain, but pleasant face. The stained white apron covered her black mid-length uniform dress. Rex glanced at her left hand; she wore no ring. What about her past? They were about the same age. She seemed to have her life together, unlike him. She wasn't his type, but something about her was attractive. Nancy wouldn't draw to someone like him, he thought, with all his baggage.

"You're figuring things out; does this have something to do with Don?" she asked.

"A little." Rex nodded.

"Don came here from Vietnam with a wife and kid about seven, eight years ago. Good folk. Worked a packing house first, then got himself a chopstick shrimp boat. He does right, you know. You ever met him?"

"Sort of," Rex said. He couldn't tell whether Nancy was prying or just being friendly. Rex was not ready to talk about his past with anyone in his new hometown. He also decided to keep his animus toward the Vietnamese private. "Much obliged, Nancy," Rex said. "Don Nguyen. Got it." He stood and placed a few bills on the table. Facing Nancy, he said, "I'll ring my boys soon. Promise."

• • •

The lightbulb at the front door burned dimly; moths circled the glow. Dung sat alone in a blue metal chair on the far end of the porch, at the edge of darkness. He had sat there for the past hour, thinking. Painful memories had filled his mind all afternoon and into the evening. Seeing Thompson for the first time in years down at the boatyard jolted him with thoughts of injustice. Tortuous recollections of the war buzzed in his head. Forget and forgive; those were the words of his wife. But could he?

Dung removed his white rubber boots, placed them by his chair, and padded across the deck in his stockinged feet. He opened the door to his house and turned off the outside light—the moths scattered to other bulbs still burning in the neighborhood.

It was dark inside and late. Dung eased open the door to his daughter's bedroom and peered inside to see her slight frame under heavy covers, outlined by a soft beam coming in through a window. He knew she was too young to remember the war. All she recognized was her new life in America. At her age, she had no interest in or desire to know her parent's past life. He would tell her when she was older, could understand, and wanted answers. He would tell her about how he, his father, and his two brothers had been commissioned in the South Vietnamese Army. He would teach her about Ho Chi Minh, the Vietcong, General Giap, the French, and the Communists. He would tell her about his country's prolonged war and how her grandfather and one of her uncles died fighting the Vietcong and the North Vietnamese. He would tell her how Americans tried to help.

Someday, he would tell her how they escaped the war in a fishing boat when she was only four years old. He would tell her how their small craft motored out to sea to avoid atrocities in the hands of the invading communist soldiers.

He knew the communist North did not pardon surviving South Vietnamese officers at the end of the war but tried them as war criminals. They sent the lucky to re-education camps—the unlucky, they executed and buried in unmarked mass graves.

Dung couldn't imagine what would have happened to his young wife and daughter if they had not escaped. He couldn't go there in his mind. Thi Anh should know someday about the human cost of war in her ancestral homeland. Eventually, he would tell her, but not now.

Dung tip-toed down the hall to the bedroom he shared with his wife. He undressed outside the door, letting his clothes pile on the pinewood floor. He crept in, pulled back the covers, and slid into bed next to Linh.

"Forgive him," Linh whispered as she rolled over to put her arm around Dung's chest.

Dung remained on his back and stared at the dark ceiling but did not respond.

"Forgive him. It was the past. Forgive him," she said.

"I should never have let him get away with it," Dung said, without looking at Linh.

"You acted as you did at the time because . . ."

"Why didn't I have him arrested?"

"... of what you thought was best. Let it go."

"He came back and stole the money. I know he did. They blamed me for this."

"Yes, I've heard this before. You made it through. We made it out. That's what matters now," Linh said.

"I suffered in Laos. That bastard did that to me."

"*Anh* Dung?"

Dung rolled away from his wife and faced the wall. For almost eight years, he feared he might run into Rex Thompson in America. But this was a big country. What were the chances? Slim, he had told himself. Tonight, rage and revenge burned in his mind. He could not turn them off—he could not scatter the thoughts circling in his head.

"I fought for my country. I fought to stay alive. I fought for you and Thi Anh," Dung murmured.

Linh pulled the sheets off her side of the bed. She swung her slender legs off the edge and sat. "I'll make tea. Come, let's talk." She rose and left the room.

Dung pulled on a robe and followed.

• • •

The heater at the Tivoli Hotel never worked right—Rex thought it did not get cold enough in Biloxi for anyone to pay it much mind. He draped a blanket over his shoulders and poured himself another half-glass of Old Crow. He replaced the fifth of bourbon on the top shelf of his closet, despite knowing he would empty the bottle by morning.

Tomorrow, if he were sober, he thought, he would call his boys. He would ask them about their Christmas and apologize for not sending presents. He would explain how busy the boat kept him and how much he wished to come for a visit. Rex had always used these same lines with the boys. Were they now old enough to see through his lies? It was time, long past the time, for him to turn himself around, stop drinking, stop running, and be the father he had hoped he could be.

Rex pulled open the nightstand drawer and found a sheet of paper under a Gideon Bible. He started to make a list, a promise, a hope—words that could reshape his life. Words which, if followed, would set him straight. Words he had written on a New Year's Day many times before.

CHAPTER 7

June 2, 1985

The sensual, soul-catching zydeco beat came to a stop just as a patter of light rain started on the red metal roof of the old Coast Guard seaplane hangar at the edge of the bay. Musicians on stage put down their fiddles, accordions, guitars, and drumsticks. A crowd of three hundred partygoers—dancing and drinking right outside the open hangar doors—came to a rest. Terrible feedback then screeched over the PA as the mayor of Biloxi, Ace Arguelles, tested the microphone. It was time to present the teenage Shrimp Queen contestants and crown the next king of the festival.

The Shrimp Fest *fais do do* was in full swing on the first Saturday in June as Biloxi celebrated the new shrimp season on Point Cadet. Boiled shrimp with corn and new potatoes, jambalaya with Andouille sausage, coleslaw, sweet tea, and beer flowed from pop-up tents surrounding the aging tarmac. A gentle warm breeze lifted off the water from the nearby channel. Tomorrow, the waterway would teem with shrimp boats and pleasure craft, decorated in red, white, and blue streamers, and lined up for the 56th Annual Blessing of the Fleet ceremony.

Biloxi traditions ran deep with folks who, for generations, had made their livelihood in the seafood industry. The previous night was a time of remembrance. At St. Michael Catholic Church, there was a mass and vigil for the many fishermen who had lost their lives in years past on the unpredictable, tempest-prone, shallow waters of the Gulf. Today was a day of celebration—with food and music and the coming together of friends and families—in anticipation of another successful shrimp season. Tomorrow would be a day of hope and prayer. A priest would lower a wreath into the bay as the shrimp fleet paraded by to receive a blessing for a safe and bountiful harvest.

Nancy sat with her sister, Susan, on folding wooden chairs with an unobstructed view of the open hangar. Susan pulled out a tiny umbrella and held it over both as the rain continued.

"Mary Kate was some excited when she found out she was going to be in the pageant this year," Susan said.

"Did you have to buy the dress?" Nancy asked.

"No, Emily—you know, the blond whose mamma and 'em live up the road a ways—wore it last year. Emily didn't even make the final four, so I don't expect anyone will even remember."

"Where's MK going next year?"

"She's fixing to go to Southern. With some friends, too."

"Nice," Nancy said.

"But she'll need some money if that's going to happen."

"If she makes Shrimp Queen, you can put that cash up," Nancy said.

"Yeah, I reckon."

Ten young ladies, called out by the mayor, then gracefully walked across the stage and stood behind him with their best beauty-queen poses. Mary Kate looked stunning with a long blue satin dress and rhinestone heels; her brown hair was pinned high on her head, exposing her slim neck. Nancy was glad Susan had insisted she close the café for the day to watch her niece compete for the title. Mayor Arguelles told the crowd how proud he was that Biloxi could produce such lovely ladies, how lucky Biloxians were to have such a stable seafood industry, and how much he was doing for the city as mayor.

"You'd think he was running again this year," Nancy said.

"He's always running, like his mouth."

With an outstretched hand, the mayor recognized and congratulated the fire chief, the city council members, the police chief, the city directors, and other members of his administration in the crowd.

"Someone get a boathook," Susan said to Nancy, straining to look around the mayor to where her daughter was standing.

The mayor eventually got around to introducing Boo Gilly, the reigning Shrimp King from the previous year. King Gilly stepped onto the stage with a scepter in hand and nudged Ace from the mic.

"It's been a wonderful twelve months for me," the Shrimp King said to the crowd. "Just want to thank all y'all for giving me this opportunity to represent the city this past year. What a lovely group of young ladies we have today, huh?" Gilly turned to face the contestants. "Give it up for these fine girls."

The crowd stood clapping, dropping their hats, and raising Solo cups of beer and tea into the air to salute the court. As if on cue, the ten young ladies, standing with one foot in front of the other, waved to the crowd by raising a white-gloved forearm, pointing fingers to the sky, and rotating cupped palms. Nancy and Susan sat again on their folding chairs. The light rain let up.

"How'd you think Momma's doing? You talk to her lately?" Nancy asked.

"No. Seems like when I visit, she don't want me around."

King Boo Gilly leaned into the microphone. "Ladies and gentlemen, boys and girls, it's that time of the day to name the queen finalists."

"You'd think after Daddy died, she'd get out, see people," Nancy said.

"Shh! Shut your mouth," Susan said to Nancy while straining to listen through the loudspeaker's static.

King Gilly called four girls, including Mary Kate, to come forward on the stage. Susan grabbed Nancy's arm and sat up in her seat. The crowd quieted. The King spoke, "This is a day these four beauties will remember for the rest of their lives. Nothing can take this accomplishment away from them. All you parents out there must be proud."

The King looked once more to four teenage girls standing next to him, and his attention seemed to drift.

Slowing his voice, he then announced with a dramatic staccato of syllables, "The 1985 Shrimp Queen is . . . Miss Mary Kate Oberman."

"That's great!" Nancy said, then she leaned over to Susan. "Congratulations. What's that make you? Queen Mother?"

"Yeah, and it makes you the *Ant* Queen."

On stage, Mary Kate lowered her head to receive a dazzling tiara.

"Queen Mother, I think you need a plastic crown, too," Nancy teased. "Guess you're going to retire the dress now, huh? No other queen-wannabes will wear it next year."

Susan smiled at her sister.

Ace Arguelles and Boo Gilly shook the hands of the new Shrimp Queen and the other young ladies in her court. The mayor then excused all girls from the dais except for Mary Kate. Ace regained the microphone and announced the name of the new 1985 Shrimp King, a balding middle-aged businessman known to most locals only as "Spider." With exaggerated theatrics, the new king accepted the crown then spun toward the crowd with his welcoming arms raised to the clouds, generating only anemic applause. The mayor knelt on one knee and presented to him a gold plastic key to the city. The new Shrimp King then turned to receive Mary Kate, who offered the back of her gloved hand for a kiss as she curtsied.

"Give enough money to the city, and anyone can be king for a weekend," Nancy opined.

"Where's your king? You seeing anyone lately?" Susan asked.

"No."

"I wouldn't recommend our new Shrimp King," Susan said, looking to the stage. "But there're plenty of others out there."

"I guess. I'm just not interested or haven't found the right one."

"Daddy?"

"Yeah."

The band beat out a tempo on the Cajun rubboard and added a melody on the fiddle as the newly-crowned Shrimp King and Queen made their way off the stage to greet their *subjects*. The *fais do do* was back swinging. Couples joined hands on the concrete apron and scooted their feet in a two-step.

"You'll find your man, Nancy."

"Perhaps. I'm just not in a hurry."

"Bless your heart; you're thirty-five years old. What're you waiting for?"

Nancy glared at her older sister. She would let her comment pass.

Mary Kate almost tripped in her floor-length dress and high-heeled shoes as she made her way across the cracked tarmac to where her mother and aunt were sitting.

"Good job, darling! Gimme some sugar," Susan said as she pulled her daughter in for a kiss on the cheek. "I knew you could do it."

"I'm so psyched. I just can't believe it," Mary Kate said.

"You look fabulous, Sweetie," Nancy said.

"Thanks, Aunt Nancy." The Shrimp Queen then turned to her mother. "They got champagne at the royal table. Can I have some, please?"

"Okay, just one glass, Queen MK. A small one."

"Yes, ma'am. Totally sweet on the prize money, huh?" Mary Kate said over her shoulder as she shuffled back into the festivities.

"One glass!" Susan shouted at her daughter, then turned to Nancy. "What about Rex?"

"Just a friend."

"Is he going to have his boat at the Blessing tomorrow?"

"Don't think so. Rex doesn't do that kind of stuff. Never seen him at the parade before," Nancy said.

Nancy looked around at the crowd and saw only Caucasian faces—French, Yugoslavian, and Spanish. She recognized the old Biloxi families: the Ladniers, Gautiers, Dukates, and Lopezes. Then there were the "viches and iches:" the Stanoviches, Barhanoviches, Mladiniches, and Treboticheses. The Vietnamese shrimpers were missing. She knew many of them were Catholic and assumed they might want to partake in the Blessing of the Fleet. But they did not. How many more seasons, she thought, before this latest group of immigrants felt welcome on the Coast?

"Does he drink?" Susan asked, bringing Nancy back into the conversation.

"Yeah. And divorced."

"Buddy drinks, but he's never been ugly," Susan said, referring to her husband and Mary Kate's stepfather.

"I know—"

A short train approached on nearby tracks and drowned out the music and conversation. Nancy held up her index finger to signal a pause. Two engines pulling a dozen boxcars, tagged with graffiti in far-off cities, rocked and rattled east toward the swing bridge. Steel wheels screeched on iron rails. Diesel fumes flooded the tarmac.

The train passed.

"I'm just so wary of getting involved with someone who could turn out like Daddy," Nancy said.

"Nobody's like that son-of-a-bitch."

"Hey, why you think the Vietnamese don't come today?" Nancy asked.

"They don't like jambalaya. That's what Buddy says."

"No, seriously, Susan, why not?"

"I don't know. Maybe they don't feel comfortable yet. Other shrimpers haven't, you know, like, gone to town to lay out the welcome mat."

"Rex don't care much for them either."

"He said that?" Susan asked.

"No, I can just tell. Maybe the war."

"What was that, ten years ago? Tell him to get over it."

"We're not that close. I'm not telling him nothing."

The band slowed the beat for the Shrimp King and Queen to take the floor. Other dancers parted for the royal couple. Watching her sixteen-year-old niece dance arm in arm with the new shrimp monarch made Nancy uncomfortable. Spider was old enough to be Mary Kate's father, typical of the Shrimp Fest royalty. Mary Kate appeared oblivious to the attention she generated in her tight-fitting blue gown, cut low in the back. Today was the last time Susan should let MK wear this one, Nancy thought. Time to retire the dress.

CHAPTER 8

August 13, 1985

Rex eased up on the throttle to bring the *Chasin' Tail* to idle speed. The outriggers stood raised as she rocked in a three-foot chop. He had towed a pair of trawls between Horn and Deer Islands for the past four hours, and it was time to haul in his catch. It had been an excellent trip so far. He hoped to top twelve thousand pounds of brown shrimp for the week with the morning's drag. The cable winches whined as Rex lowered green nets, bulging with shrimp, onto the deck.

"Jake, watch your head," Rex shouted above the noise to his son.

Pigeon grabbed the bag tie on the port net and pulled hard on the looped half-hitched knot to release a wave of translucent crustaceans and silver baitfish onto the deck. Jake emptied the starboard net in the same manner. The boys then guided the trawls and tackle back over the side as Rex lowered the rigging to steady the boat.

Jake raised his hand and slapped the back of Pigeon's head. "Frickin' awesome. Huh?"

"Bite me, dickweed." Pigeon flicked his blond hair back and elbowed his brother in the side.

Both teenagers then sat on the slimy deck with their legs outstretched

in front of the puddle of shrimp. It was time to sort the catch and store it below on ice. They both worked to pull out the market shrimp and fill the orange plastic mesh baskets at their side. Rex joined in on the picking. These were beautiful browns in the 20 to 30 count-per-pound range, making this one of his most successful trips this season.

"Dad, we want to stay here," Jake said.

"Nope." Rex shook his head.

Pigeon started to protest. "But—"

"You're going back to your mamma's next week. Y'all got school."

Jake stopped sorting and waved a handful of shrimp. "We can school here, live with you. We can help on the boat."

It was the first time Jake and Pigeon had come for the summer to live with their dad in Biloxi. Rex was thrilled to have them. They were young men now and eager to prove their worth to their father. When Deborah had phoned at the end of the school year to see if he was in any condition to take the boys for a few months, he lied. He was still staying at the Tivoli Hotel and having difficulty staying sober. But the shrimp season was getting started. He would have to back off the bottle if he were to get out on the water and earn any money. The bank had a lien on the shrimper; he had bills to pay.

"Sure, Debbie . . ." Rex hesitated on the phone. "Can you git 'em out?" He didn't want to admit to her he didn't own a car.

"Howard can run 'em," Deborah said, referring to her brother. "He's gotta go to Florida anyways, week coming up."

"Okay, yeah, that'll work."

"Rex, can you handle this shit? Can you get yourself right for a few months, be a goddamn daddy to your boys?"

"Sure, Deb." Rex wondered if the doubts he had in his mind came through in his voice.

"Despite your being an asshole, they somehow still love ya," she said.

"I'll do my best."

"Just take 'em two months."

"Send some spending money, Debbie. I want 'em to have a good time."

The receiver went dead. Rex listened to the dial tone and thought of the times he had failed his family. When had his life come apart? Or did he ever have it together? Was it the war? Was he screwed up before he ever left for Nam? Had he been screwed up his entire life? He had left a long trail of broken promises, heartbreak, and shit.

Rex put the receiver back in the cradle and just stood in the phone booth. Heavy rain fell, and he squeezed in tight under the small overhang. Taking the boys for a few months could be the turning point in his life. It would be a fantastic summer, he thought. They could sleep on the boat. He would teach them to shrimp—man's work—and maybe they could reconnect. Perhaps it would all work out.

Rex lowered the shrimp through the main hatch into the ice hold and said nothing more about the boys staying on after the summer. Jake lifted a wide-mouth shovel and started to scoop up what they had left on the deck and toss it overboard. The boat pulled forward as shovelfuls of discarded finfish dotted the water's surface in the boat's wake. Laughing gulls dropped from the sky on each patch of dead croakers, grunts, and menhaden. The birds picked out the choice morsels before the mess sank to where redfish, speckled trout, and sharks had their turn. Finally, the blue crabs on the muddy bottom got what was left.

Alone in the pilothouse, Rex grabbed the wheel and spun it several times to port. He pushed the throttle forward. It was time to return to the dock and unload their catch. It had been a great summer with his boys, and he hated to see them go. He had never considered they would stay more than a few months. For most of their lives, he had not been a good father to them. But in the past two months, he had changed for the better. Could he keep it up? Could he stay sober? Could he provide for his sons and guide them into adulthood better than his own father had? Rex longed to have Jake and Pigeon close. He wanted to be in their lives; now it seemed they wanted it, too. If they stayed, he would have to rent a place to live and get a car—more mouths to feed. Maybe for the rest of the season, the boys could help on the boat, weekends, and holidays.

Rex shouted out the pilothouse door toward the main deck, "One semester, that's it! Either of you dicks around in school, y'all both going back to your mamma's." Rex stepped back inside, placed one hand on the wheel, and picked up the VHF mic to contact the dock and sell his shrimp. A small smile spread over his weathered cheeks.

• • •

Don Nguyen watched from the pier as the red and green boat made its way up the Back Bay Channel. He knew this boat and its owner well. Don was familiar with Rex Thompson's drinking, gambling, and financial snags. Even though they lived in the same town and shrimped in the same waters, Don had avoided Rex ever since he first saw him at the boatyard two-and-one-half years ago. Don was not one to forgive easily; he thought it best to make sure their paths did not cross. But his continued anger toward the pain he thought Rex caused him in Vietnam had eaten into his soul. Linh had begged him to forgive and to let go. Now, as the *Chasin' Tail* was pulling in next to his boat, the *Tien Hai*, Don thought perhaps it was time. Time to make amends. Time to let go of his anger.

Don was surprised by a sudden thought of violence when he caught a glimpse of Rex standing in the pilothouse. He imagined running a Ka-Bar up under Rex's ribs. *Stick him like a pig*. Violent memories then flashed through his mind. He saw himself sitting in a bamboo cage, taunted by his North Vietnamese captors. Flies and the stench of death lingered in the air. Wounds on his back and legs festered with maggots.

Sunlight bounced off the water surrounding the *Chasin' Tail* as it maneuvered in a narrow inlet near the dock. The vessel's diesel engine whined as it reversed into the slip. Don saw two teenage boys scramble about the deck, dropping bumpers off the side and preparing dock lines—boys the same age as the enemy soldiers who took him as a prisoner, just over the Laotian border, fourteen years ago.

Don should have died when the North Vietnamese Army ambushed his platoon along a jungle trail. Eight men, including the platoon sergeant, perished with bullet wounds to the head and chest while facing the enemy. These were heroes he could never forget. Four men and himself were left pinned behind fallen logs. The NVA encircled their position, and soon they were taking fire from several directions. It was midday but dark under the jungle canopy. Communication with the rest of his company was cut. Within minutes, they recognized, they would expend their ammunition. The NVA understood this as well and put just enough pressure on them to keep them firing into the jungle. The end would come soon enough.

The North Vietnamese squad had no use for prisoners, especially for an officer of the Army of the Republic of Vietnam. Captain Dung knew what each of his remaining four men was thinking as their defenses crumbled: save one bullet for themselves. The next soldier to die bit the muzzle of his M1 carbine and tripped the trigger. Two more men followed. Dung waited for his last man to run out of ammunition. He saw no way out. Dung ripped the rank insignia off his uniform and buried them with his empty sidearm in the jungle detritus under his feet. Enemy bullets seared the humid air above his head and exploded into wet tree trunks. Dung's last man fired his final round into the roof of his mouth and collapsed.

Don watched Rex jump off the boat and engage the harbormaster in what appeared to be a dispute. He was too far away to hear the conversation but could see each man stiffen his spine and gesture with outstretched arms. Someone would get pushed into the water if one of them didn't back down, he thought. He noticed Rex look at his two boys, who were watching the argument, and step aside.

Back in the jungle of Southeast Asia, Dung couldn't do it. He held a rifle muzzle with both hands under his chin with a stick through the trigger guard. *He was a coward.* The shooting stopped, and the forest was quiet for a moment. Vietnamese voices, in a language, shared on both sides of the battlefield, then surrounded him. Soon they would take his honor with a bullet in the back of his head. He closed his eyes. A vision flashed in his mind of his young wife Linh, combing her silky black hair and putting lotion on her white legs and arms—the sweet scent of flowers on her skin.

A twig snapped. His eyes opened.

The first of the NVA emerged from the jungle.

"Stop, I with American!" Dung shouted in English, knowing he would not be understood but perhaps buying some time.

"I with American GI Special Forces," Dung continued in English with his hands up in the air. He then repeated himself in Vietnamese while gauging his soon-to-be captors or executioners; he did not know which.

Don looked again at the *Chasin' Tail* and saw the boys load shrimp into a galvanized steel hopper. He could see it would be a big payday for Rex. Perhaps this was why he was able to defuse the harbormaster. He wanted to confront Rex right then and tell him what had happened to him in the war: how he had taken the blame for the missing cash, been stripped of his position in Da Nang, and sent across the Laotian border on a suicide mission. He wanted to tell him about the ten months, spent as a prisoner, shuffled from one makeshift camp to another in the jungles of Laos, how he escaped and worked his way east through the highlands to safety, and how he was sent back to the fight at Cam Lo in 1972.

Don watched the boys unload the boat. He knew Linh was right. The only way to find peace within himself was to forgive Rex and others. Could he do it without a confrontation? He did not know. Don caught Rex's glance in his direction, and their eyes met for a brief second. He sensed the momentary opening of an emotive shutter—a mutual connection—then he turned and walked home.

CHAPTER 9

November 12, 1987

The shattering of glass and an immediate explosion cracked Lam Trung out of a dream and flipped him out of his hammock onto the pilothouse deck. Confused, Lam scanned the compartment as he tried to make sense of what had just happened. Undulating yellow light bounced off the boats tied up next to the *Tien Hai,* filling the windows with an unnatural glow.

Lam spun his small frame around, pulling himself up, and raced to the open doorway. Flames leaped from the back of his boat, consuming a canvas tarp suspended over the deck. He returned into the pilothouse and flipped on the VHF radio.

"Mayday! Mayday! Mayday!" Lam screamed into the mic. "*Đây là tàu Tiên Hải tại bến tàu, Fit* Street. *Tàu cháy!* Mayday! *Tiên Hải, Fit* Street. Mayday! *Tiên Hải, Fit* Street. Mayday! *Tiên Hải, Fit* Street. *Tàu cháy! Tàu cháy! Tàu cháy!*"

Lam grabbed a fire extinguisher mounted on the bulkhead and jumped through the doorway. Flames licked at his bare feet and legs. He emptied the extinguisher, spraying foam onto the deck before him with a negligible effect. He backpedaled into the wheelhouse and started up the diesel engine to power the main water pumps. Climbing through the cabin's starboard window, he retrieved a two-inch rubber hose coiled on the foredeck. Lam then inched toward the boat's stern and saw that the blaze had engulfed the entire deck. Heat burned at his face. He opened the nozzle and sprayed water into the inferno. Flames shot upward as the stream blew burning gasoline into the air. Lam then directed his spray to the portions of the boat, not yet ablaze. Pungent smoke clogged the air as old tires, hanging from the side of the shrimper, lighted and burned. Fire touched the nylon nets hanging dry in the rigging above, and they flashed like giant lanterns in the night sky.

Sirens wailed, and soon red blinking lights reflected off the other boats in the harbor before being lost into the darkness of the bay. Firemen descended on the *Tien Hai* from both sides and flooded the burning deck with foam. In a matter of minutes, they had extinguished the blaze.

• • •

Lam crouched on the dock, sitting on his heels. He watched a half-dozen firemen in tan suits explore the boat, looking for remaining hotspots. A police cruiser's blue lights appeared nearby and flashed out of sync with the fire engine's red. A Biloxi officer emerged and engaged one of the firemen.

Don Nguyen drove up to the scene, got out of a yellow Datsun B210 hatchback, and stood next to Lam Trung, who remained down. Both men stared at the ghostly image of the boat covered in a blanket of white foam and lit up by a random strobe of red and blue.

"What happened?" Don asked his pilot in Vietnamese.

Lam responded, "I don't know, *Anh* Dung. An explosion woke me up while I was sleeping up front. Good thing I wasn't below deck. It's hot tonight, and I hung a hammock to get air."

"Where did it start?"

"In the back, on the deck. On the deck, not inside. I started the diesel to spray water. I'm not sure that was a great idea," Lam said. "I'm sorry about your boat."

"It's just a boat. I have lost boats before. My friends and family, those are who I no longer wish to lose."

Lam stood and faced Don. "This is my fault," Lam said.

"No. Do not speak of that."

The police officer approached the two men and held out a broken glass shard—the neck of a quart bottle. "Found this on the deck," he said. "Other fragments are scattered around the winch. It's a Molotov cocktail, a firebombing."

It surprised Don that someone would target his boat. Several years ago, there had been a few skirmishes between American and Vietnamese fishermen on the Mississippi waters, but he was never directly involved. Local shrimpers took offense to the Vietnamese for leaving the oyster plants and going after shrimp. The immigrants didn't play by the same rules. A language barrier impaired their understanding of the written regulations and the unwritten laws of open water.

Throughout the Gulf Coast, as soon as a Vietnamese family could get enough money to build a small boat, the whole clan would work it as much as twenty-four hours a day. Pooled profits bought new and larger vessels. The second and third-generation American shrimpers found it hard to compete with their new Asian neighbors. Tensions flared, and the fishermen often settled conflicts with violence.

But, Don thought, things had settled down in the last year or two. He did not expect his boat to be the recipient of such an attack—he had a good relationship of mutual respect with the other local shrimpers.

Don then spoke to the policeman in English, "I'm the *Tien Hai* owner, my name is Don Nguyen, n-g-u-y-e-n. This is my employee, Lam, l-a-m, Trung, t-r-u-n-g, who was staying on the boat tonight."

The officer wrote their names in a small notepad and asked, "Any reason someone did this? You piss-off anyone lately?"

Lam shook his head.

Don responded, "No, we have no enemies, just friends. We like all the fishermen here."

"You know people can only git pushed 'round so far before they'll resort to something like this shit. Never had these problems ten years ago when people 'round here seemed to know their place."

"Thank you, Officer, for looking into this," Don said. "Perhaps it was an accident or maybe just some kids doing things they shouldn't."

The officer said, "You downplaying this? Those firemen near about hurt themselves responding to your fire."

"I take this seriously, like you. I just don't wish to cause any trouble here," Don said.

"You already did. Both y'all come to the station tomorrow and give a statement. You best come together if your little helper here don't speak English good." The policeman put the glass shard into an evidence bag and returned to the boat.

In Vietnamese, Lam said, "*Anh* Dung, I have something else to say. Last week, when I was dragging down in Chandeleur, the *Renée Sue,* you know from Louisiana, crossed my wake and picked up my trawl. I had to cut the lead line, and I lost a net. I didn't want to tell you, and I was going to replace it. That shrimper had been bothering me all day. They acted like they owned the ocean. I was just trying to keep to myself and avoid them. Then I see her on the port side, pulling her trawls right into my path. I had the right-of-way, and that boat should have slowed down or come off. That is when she cut behind me so close that one of my nets got snagged. The *Renée Sue* fouled, dead in the water. I cut my tackle and got out of there fast. I think if they or their friends could have gotten to me, then I would be dead. They saw my boat. Ask Quang, he'll tell you," referring to his deckhand. "I don't know what they were thinking. Those bastards from Louisiana set the fire. I'm sure."

Don put his hand on his shoulder. "Lam, you brought honor to the *Tien Hai* and yourself. Today we were slapped on one side of the face; tomorrow, we do nothing but present the other side."

CHAPTER 10

August 30, 1993

A navy-blue Ford Crown Victoria with government plates drove down a long two-track under a canopy of loblolly pines and southern magnolias. Overgrown brush lined the narrow road. The car tracks exposed ancient oyster shells on the high spots; muddy water filled the low. Fred Necaise's thoughts turned briefly from solving a murder to cleaning his car after a quarter of a mile drive on this old shell road.

Agent Fred Necaise worked for the Mississippi Bureau of Investigation and was the principal detective on the *Miss Anh* and Don Nguyen case. Today, he was going to an old fishing camp on Back Bay's low-lying shore to follow a lead. What he understood so far was that the *Miss Anh* had been intentionally scuttled two weeks prior when a cable yanked the driveshaft out of its housing, sinking the trawler within minutes. Flooding water trapped the boat's owner, Don Nguyen, below deck. His son-in-law survived. Agent Necaise had only a sixty-foot length of a quarter-inch cable and a brief list of potential suspects to begin his investigation. He wanted to talk to the boat's previous owner, but nobody he spoke to had seen him on the coast for several months. Fred Necaise was driving out to see where Rex Thompson used to live.

Asbestos shingles covered the exterior of the small square house, raised on three-foot cinder block pilings. Unpainted wooden steps led up to a tiny landing and a screened front door. The camp's back faced one hundred yards of muddy land that gave way to salt grass and the open water of Back Bay. Saw palmettos filled areas of moist ground where sunlight filtered through the pine trees.

Necaise pulled his car into a small opening in the woods near the house and noticed tire tracks in the mud. Someone had recently parked a vehicle there. He was just asking questions today, he thought, looking for clues. He stepped out of his car and climbed the slick wooden steps to knock on the door.

A faded yellow curtain pulled back at the edge of the front window. Necaise heard a chain being placed inside the door as someone released the deadbolt. The face of a tall young man with long brown hair appeared in the crack.

"Agent Necaise, Mississippi Department of Investigation," he said and held out his badge. He wore a dark blue suit with a white shirt and black tie. "I'm looking for Rex Thompson."

"He's not here," the man said.

Necaise shoved the toe of his oxford up against the door. "I just want to ask some questions. Can you come out?"

"Yeah."

Necaise pulled his shoe back.

Jake closed the door and released the security chain, then stepped out toward the agent. Nothing to hide. No way they could connect him and Pigeon to the *Miss Anh*. Nobody could have seen them in the skiff that night; it was too dark. Even if someone had spotted the boat, there were hundreds of johnboats just like theirs scattered over the coast. The brothers had been careful to use an old cable and leave no fingerprints. After running the skiff, they had turned it over in the yard. Two weeks of tropical rainstorms had washed away any footprints around the boat to indicate recent use.

Facing each other, Jake and Fred Necaise stood the same height.

"What's up, Officer?" Jake asked. He'd known this moment would come.

"I'm looking for Rex Thompson. I understand that until eight months ago, he owned the *Miss Anh*."

"*Chasin' Tail*," Jake spat.

Necaise scribbled on a notepad. "Right, are you one of his sons?"

"Yup, Jake Thompson," he said and stuck his arm out for an awkward handshake.

Necaise took his hand. "Where is your brother Peter?"

"Pigeon, ain't nobody calls 'im Peter."

"Right."

"Went to the store this morning, I think."

"Right. I want to ask your dad some questions about the boat. When was the last time you saw him?"

"January, February, don't know. 'Bout eight months past."

Necaise had gone through this line of questioning before, hundreds of times. It was like a script. "Where did he go?"

"Don't know."

"Why did he leave?"

"Don't know, man."

"Have you talked to him recently?" Necaise acted as if he were writing essential facts, but he already knew the responses.

"Nope, not a word." Jake looked into Agent Necaise's eyes. These were all truths and easy to say.

"Do you know why your dad sold the boat?"

Jake knew why. His dad had started to drink heavily about a year after the brothers moved to Biloxi. Jake was fifteen, and Pigeon was fourteen when they left their mother's place in Texas. The first year in Mississippi was cool. They enrolled at Magnolia High, made new friends, and even tried out for the football team. On weekends and school nights, the boys helped their father on the boat. Rex seemed proud of his sons. Everything was working out well.

But then Rex found the bottle once more. At first, it was just on an occasional night when the boys had something else to do. Soon, he added Jim Beam to his coffee and iced tea. On weekends, he began to disappear.

Within a year, Jake and Pigeon had dropped out of high school to help work the boat. They pitched in where their dad came up short. More than once, they borrowed a friend's car to run into town in the early morning to retrieve their daddy from a bar, a casino, Waffle House, or the city lockup. They often found him smelling of liquor and piss, slumped over a table, or lying on the sidewalk with empty pockets.

"He didn't sell it. They all took it." Jake gazed to the woods and down the drive, looking for his brother's return.

"My understanding is the bank repossessed the boat because your father didn't make payments on a note."

"Not sure 'bout that. You gotta ask Dad."

Of course, he didn't pay the note, Jake thought. A year ago, dockside gambling opened in Biloxi, and the temptation was just too much for their father. Loose slots stoked old habits, and before long, he was hooked. Poker, craps, roulette, bourbon, and smokes consumed him.

"Do you know how I can get a hold of your father?" Necaise asked.

"Nope, don't know." Jake shook his head.

From darkening skies, a clap echoed across the water. Sheets of rain began to obscure the pine trees on the bay's far shoreline. A cool breeze blew to an updraft as the thunderhead approached. Both men realized a soaking downpour would descend upon them in minutes. The storm would last only a half-hour or so, but it was time to seek shelter.

Necaise had come to the house to find Rex; he was not prepared today to question his sons. He pulled out a business card and handed it to Jake. "My number is here. Call me if you hear from your father."

Fred Necaise turned to hustle down the steps and back to his car. He did not see Jake give him a two-fingered scout salute or hear him whisper, "Fuck you."

Necaise ducked into his sedan as the first large drops of rain fell through the trees. He switched on his headlights and wipers, turned the car around in the clearing, and drove down the curved drive. The undercarriage of the vehicle bottomed out on the strip of grass between the muddy tracks. He knew his partner at the office would never let up if he got his car stuck and had to call a wrecker. The rear wheels finally found traction on the oyster shells, and Necaise turned left on Bay

Road, returning to the office just as the sun poked through the clouds again.

• • •

"Where the hell ya been?" Jake fired off as Pigeon walked into the front room with a bucket of fried chicken in one hand and a Styrofoam cup in the other. Jake had been mulling over Agent Necaise's visit while lying on a worn and stained couch, the only significant piece of furniture in the house. When he had heard Pigeon drive up, he got up to confront him at the door.

"Fuck you," Pigeon said as he pushed Jake aside with the back of his forearm.

"Listen, man. Some state investigator dude came looking for Dad."

"So, ain't that what we, like, expected? What'd ya say?"

Jake pulled out the card and handed it to Pigeon. "I told 'im we had no idea where he was. Real easy, ya know, 'cuz it's the truth."

"That's it? All the mother-fucker wanted to know?" Pigeon scanned the card.

"Damn right." Jake walked over to a small dinette and slid a metal chair out to sit.

Pigeon put the chicken bucket and his drink on the table and sat in another chair. He pulled out a greasy drumstick and ate the meat off the bone.

"So, what's up now?" Pigeon asked. "What ya going to do? We knew someone was going come 'round, shake us." He took a big drink from his straw. "They can't prove shit. You know that."

"Still, didn't take long for the bastards to start snooping. I got the feeling this Necaise guy already knew Dad was gone. Hell, he knew your got-damn name." Jake leaned back in his chair so he could reach behind and open the icebox.

"No, you're not." Pigeon shook his head with half a drumstick sticking out of his mouth. "That's my shit."

"Bull crap," Jake said as he pulled out a can of beer.

"I said, that's my beer."

"Okay, you can't be a smart ass about this. Remember? Keep your trap shut. Nobody but us knows. Leave it that way, and we're clean."

"What ya icing my grill for? I ain't said shit."

"Good." Jake popped the beer and took a sip. He looked around inside the camp. The sofa sat up against a wall at the far end of the main room. The dinette and a small kitchen were at the other end. Yellow curtains hung closed from flimsy rods over three small windows. A window cooler, rattling out chilled air, filled the fourth. Since the flood of Hurricane Andrew, an indoor-outdoor carpet covered the plywood floor. Two small bedrooms and a bathroom came off a narrow hallway between the couch and the kitchen. Black mold crept up the inside door and window trim. The place was dank.

They didn't own the house. Their father paid rent every month to a lady for a while. After he left town, nobody came looking for more. Jake and Pigeon just stayed; they had nowhere else to go.

Jake looked at his brother. He had fried chicken crumbs and grease on his fingers and face. Pigeon wiped his hands and mouth on his shirt before walking back to the toilet.

"Amber's coming, few minutes," Pigeon said as he peed with the door open.

"What, you shitting me? That's not cool." Jake tipped forward in his chair, and the front legs banged the thin flooring.

"We're just shooting the bull. I'm not doing that shit no more," Pigeon said while shuffling down the hall and zipping his shorts.

"We're in a bit of a mess right now, Pigeon, if you haven't noticed. Need to keep to ourselves, lie low for a few weeks."

"Amber's fly. I can't like fucking sit around here all day long."

"I don't believe ya. Thought you dropped that shit when Dad left," Jake said.

"I did. Chill, would ya? I'm not doing no crystal."

Jake got up and stood in Pigeon's face. "I don't fucking believe ya."

"Calling me a liar?" Pigeon leaned in.

"I'm calling it what it is, Pige." Jake pushed his forefinger into Pigeon's chest. "Every time I see that meth bitch, she's amped. She's damn trouble."

"I'm not doing crap." Pigeon shoved Jake with both hands and stepped back. "Told you."

"You don't need to mess with her; she's already got a boyfriend."

"We're just buds, okay? We like to hang," Pigeon said. "He's cool with it."

"If that slut's coming, I'm leaving." Jake grabbed the keys off the counter and stepped to the door. "I can't believe this bull crap. It's not the time to git involved in this shit."

"Fuck off."

The screen door slammed shut behind Jake as he alighted the steps, tossed the empty beer can at the house, and jumped into an old model Ford Ranger. Jake started the engine, pulled the truck into reverse, kicked up mud, and backed around the clearing. He needed space. Jake was losing control of his brother. Muddy water splashed into the palmettos as the Ranger sped down the drive.

• • •

Agent Necaise sat in an upholstered chair facing Anh and her new husband, Timmy. The pair sat at each end of a sofa, on the other side of a dark wooden coffee table. Anh and Timmy Truong occasionally looked at him but said nothing. Necaise noticed the low table in front of him had intricate oriental figures, flowers, and dragons on its legs and skirt. He thought about the effort it took for someone to hand-carve these ornaments. Necaise looked around the sitting room. Up against the far wall were several wreaths on wire stands, the type florists made up for funerals. The flowers drooped on their stems, and brown petals littered the carpet. Conspicuous bright ribbons and cards clung to the faded arrangements. The room smelled of flowers and curry.

On a side table next to Necaise was a framed photo of Linh and Don. She wore a bright blue Asian-looking dress with a high neckline and a slit in the fabric from her ankles to her thigh. Don wore a tux with a white boutonniere and had his arm around Linh's waist. A wedding, Mardi Gras ball, or New Year's party, Necaise wondered. He had never met Don Nguyen, but Don appeared to be someone he wished to have known from his engaging smile in the photo.

Necaise glanced again at the young couple sitting at each end of the sofa and wondered why they would be seated so far apart. Wouldn't they want to touch and comfort each other? He suspected he had entered a culture of which he knew little. Anh had just lost her father, a detective was in her mother's house, and she sat on the couch, separate, with her knees together and her hands folded on her lap. She was approximately twenty, maybe a few years older, with a delicate oval-shaped face. She dressed American, but her manners were foreign. Timmy, tall and thin, had an angular jawline. He sat the same way as Anh. Nobody talked.

Necaise looked toward the kitchen door, expecting Mrs. Nguyen to return, and noticed a Latin crucifix on the wall. The twelve-inch wooden cross held a realistic-looking resin model of Jesus Christ. Painted red blood dripped from the figure's forehead, flank, hands, and feet. Necaise was uncomfortable with the deathly image, especially today when planning to question the deceased's family.

Linh entered the room from the kitchen with her gaze fixed to the floor. She held a bamboo tray of shortbread cookies arranged on a white paper doily and a steaming cup of coffee. She placed the coffee and cookies on the table in front of Necaise and bowed her head.

"Mr. Necaise, cream and sugar?" she asked in a small voice.

"No, black. Thank you." Necaise answered.

He noticed her eyes were puffy, and she had a faint smudge of dark eyeliner along the outer corner of her lower lids and over her prominent cheekbones. Linh wore her hair up in a bun and off the high collar of her buttoned-up white tunic blouse. White, loose-fitting pants danced about her slender legs as she walked.

Linh sat in the remaining upholstered chair directly under the crucifix, facing the coffee table. She clasped her hands and crossed her ankles.

Necaise took a sip of his coffee, looked at the shortbread, and wondered how long he could hold off on eating a few. His wife was always after him to drop a few pounds. He would try to resist unless he felt rude for not eating at least one.

Necaise looked alternately at Linh, Anh, and Timmy. "I'm so sorry for your loss, and I appreciate your time. As I said, I'm an investigator with the state police, and I work with the Biloxi Police Department. I understand you have previously spoken to them, but I need to ask a few more questions."

Linh and Anh gave a slight nod. They said nothing.

"Your husband Don, his given name was Dung, is that correct?" Necaise asked Linh.

Linh made another slight nod.

"Did Don have any problems with anyone you know of?"

Linh shook her head, then wiped her eyes with a small towel. It was not yet her time to reveal secrets from the past.

"Anybody ever threatened your husband, Mrs. Nguyen?"

"No," Linh answered. She looked at Anh.

Necaise turned to Timmy and Anh. "It is my understanding your father, father-in-law, bought the boat from the bank as a wedding present for you two. Is that correct?"

Timmy nodded. "Mr. Don actually owned the boat and was going to sell it to us over time. He was going to teach me how to run it. We hadn't taken it out fishing yet, just working it over." Timmy turned to Anh, glancing at her for the first time Necaise had noticed since he had come to the house.

"My father-in-law had four other shrimpers that he ran here in Biloxi," Timmy said. "He came to Biloxi with Miss Linh and Anh after the war and gradually started buying boats. He was a good fisherman and good at business. Everyone liked him. Everyone wanted to work for him."

"You saw nothing unusual on the night the boat sank, isn't that what you told the police?" Necaise asked.

"Yes, sir," Timmy responded.

Necaise put his coffee on the table and glanced at a notebook to review his questions. "Nothing you can think of that was odd or seemed out of place in the days before?"

Timmy shook his head. "Nothing."

"Why did you and Mr. Nguyen have the boat anchored in the bay that night?"

"We were checking it out to get a feel for it, you know. We worked the rigging, ran the generator and pumps. Just seeing how it handled at anchor overnight," Timmy said.

"Mr. Truong, why was it that Mr. Nguyen was down in the engine compartment at the time the vessel sank?"

"He was going to adjust the injection timing. He said that the firing was a little off. The day before, the diesel ran rough."

Necaise had an idea what Timmy was talking about, and he assumed Mr. Nguyen was in the engine room for repairs. "How about you, Mrs. Nguyen? Anything you can think of that I should follow up on?" Necaise picked up a cookie and took a bite.

Linh looked up from the floor and shook her head.

"Okay, it looks like someone sabotaged the *Miss Anh*. They wanted her sunk. I'm not sure they expected Mr. Nguyen to drown. Nevertheless, this is still a murder, and we are treating this investigation as such. We don't have a motive yet. It's a hard case. My department has a list of potential suspects to question, and we are working on this as we speak." Necaise grabbed one more shortbread cookie as he stood to leave. "We will find out who did this. If you think of anything, anything at all that might help us in the investigation, please let me know. Again, I'm so sorry for your loss. You have my number."

Timmy and Anh shook Agent Necaise's hand. Linh held her distance and dropped her chin into a subtle nod. Timmy walked the investigator out to his car.

At the navy-blue sedan, Timmy volunteered, "Miss Linh has more to say. Be patient, and she will come to you when she is ready."

"What's that?"

"I don't know the whole story, but I believe that Mr. Don and Miss Linh were connected to Rex Thompson, you know the guy who owned the boat before us, maybe as far back as the war. They never talked to me about him or what happened in Vietnam. There was just something about the boat, and Mr. Thompson, that made Mr. Don uncomfortable. The Nguyens are private people, and they keep their problems close."

"How long did you know Mr. Nguyen?"

"Five or six years, ever since Anh and I became friends."

"Has Anh ever mentioned Mr. Thompson to you?" Necaise asked.

"No. I don't think she knows him."

Agent Necaise took out another card and wrote his direct extension on the back. "Please have Mrs. Nguyen call me when she is ready."

CHAPTER 11

September 1, 1993

"Harbormaster?" Agent Necaise asked a boy about twelve at the waterfront, sitting on a white freezer chest in the shade of an elevated building.

"Yeah, up the stairs," the boy said. "Sir, you a cop?"

Necaise thought the youngster looked Asian American with a dark complexion, long thin eyes partially hidden by black bangs, and a distinctly Roman nose. East meets West. Kind of what was happening in the Biloxi shrimp business, he thought. A mixing of peoples and cultures resulted from an unpopular war fought two decades ago in a far-off corner of the world.

"Sort of. I'm an investigator. I work with the cops."

"You here because of the boat?"

"Yes, son."

The boy hopped off the chest and stood to face the agent.

"I know Timmy and Anh. Didn't know Mr. Don much. He seemed like a nice man. Everyone liked 'im," the boy said.

"You've been working here all summer?"

"Yes, sir, selling bait. Last summer, too."

"You ever seen a man by the name of Rex Thompson or his sons? They owned the boat before Mr. Nguyen bought it," Necaise said.

The young man wore a stained T-shirt, stretched out in the neck. He had tucked his slim cotton pants—too small in the waist and butt—into white rubber fishing boots, which came up to his mid-calf. The boy was as tall as Necaise.

"Didn't know 'im. Heard he was a drunk and just left Biloxi after he lost his boat. I didn't see much of the sons after that either. Used to see 'em sometimes but didn't know 'em. You think they sank the *Miss Anh*?"

"I'm not saying that, son. I'm just asking questions, just trying to figure out why someone would want to scuttle a boat."

"Mister, most folk around here don't think someone wanted to kill nobody, you know, drowning Mr. Don. They just didn't want nobody to have the boat. That's why they sunk it."

"I see. Is this what you think, too?" Necaise asked.

"Yes, sir."

"Why do you guess they wouldn't want Mr. Nguyen and Timmy to have the boat?"

"Jealous. Maybe jealous of the Vietnamese," the boy said.

"Do you think that's still a problem here?"

"Not much, but I see it now and then. I see it from both sides. My momma is from Saigon. Daddy's Italian, Keesler Air Force, retired."

"Did your folks meet in Vietnam?" Necaise asked.

"No, fishing rodeo. Not sure what my mom was doing there. She hates fishing. Me and my dad love it. You fish?"

"I have, sometimes."

"We love it. Specks, redfish, flounder."

"I see—nice talking to you, son. I'm going up to meet the harbormaster now." Necaise gave him a card.

"Black drum, sheepshead, mullet, hardheads, croakers."

"If you find out anything on the boat, you tell the harbormaster, and he'll call me. Okay?"

"Sharks, too."

The boy hopped back up on the freezer and studied the embossed seal and silver lettering on the official-looking card.

"Thanks for the help," Necaise said and turned to climb the exposed concrete stairs to the harbormaster's office.

"Pigeon and Jake done it," the boy called out.

Necaise stopped halfway up the stairs, studied the boy for a long moment, and then resumed his climb.

• • •

"Come in," Morley said from behind his desk. He had been expecting Agent Necaise after a call earlier in the day. Of course, he wanted to help with the investigation; everyone did.

"Agent Necaise, Mississippi Department of Investigation." He handed the harbormaster a card.

"Please come in, sit. Still hot out there—you'd expect it should be fall weather by now." Morley stood and extended his hand to the agent, exposing wet armpit stains on his tight-fitting polyester shirt.

Necaise unbuttoned the front of his coat and sat in a sturdy wooden chair. The type of chair his elementary school teacher in Picayune had years ago. A hard and uncomfortable chair. He would not be staying long, he hoped.

"This is about the sinking of the *Miss Anh* and Mr. Nguyen, huh?" Morley asked as he plopped into an enormous reddish-brown leather armchair with brass tack accents and leaned back. Morley had a big round face and a bad comb-over of graying blond hair to cover his balding scalp. A Band-Aid was stuck high on his freckled forehead.

Large windows with white horizontal vinyl blinds pulled up to various levels surrounded the harbormaster's office. Necaise took in the magnificent view. To the north, he could see up Back Bay to where the channel narrowed and the rivers emptied. To the east were small grassy islands, splitting the open water. The rotting hull of an oyster punt sat half-submerged on the edge of the largest island. The sun-bleached white paint of the abandoned shell, a spoil of a long-forgotten tropical storm, stood out against the dark green salt grass.

"Yes, I've got questions, and I'm hoping you can assist," Necaise said. Then he couldn't help but look out the windows facing south, out to where the *Miss Anh* had sunk. "That's where it happened, isn't it?"

Morley and Necaise got up from their chairs and walked over to the south windows.

"See that square channel marker, the green one to the left of the tree line on Deer Island? Right beyond there," Morley said, gesturing with his finger. "It sank in fourteen feet of water."

Necaise was familiar with the details of the sinking. He had spent hours in the recovered vessel where it sat on a barge in the Pascagoula River. He had climbed through the pilothouse, galley, and sleeping berths looking for clues. He had lowered himself into the engine room where they found the body of Don Nguyen. He had felt the cold, greasy driveshaft coming from the diesel engine and studied where it was bent and pulled from its housing. He had stuck his arm through the melon-size rent in the bottom of the wooden hull where the water had rushed in so fast Don Nguyen could not escape.

"Right," Necaise said. "Not too far from shore, was it?"

"No, real close, in fact."

The men sat back down; Necaise's wooden chair creaked.

"Tell me what you know about the *Chasin' Tail*. Did you know Rex Thompson well?" Necaise asked. He crossed his legs and put a notepad on his knee.

"Everyone had problems with him and his two sons," Morley said. "He came here from Texas somewhere about eighty-two or three. He brought his boat. People all called it the *Christmas Craft* or something like that, you know because it was red and green. I suppose Timmy and Don were fixing to repaint when they hauled it out next."

Necaise scribbled on his notepad.

Morley continued, "He was a drunk, Thompson was. A good shrimper when he was sober but couldn't keep himself dry. His sons came to live with him one summer when they was high school age. They just stayed, never moved back to their mamma's."

"Texas?"

"Yeah, I think so," Morley said. "Not really good kids. I don't reckon they finished school, and their daddy didn't seem to care. Maybe he cared but couldn't do nothing about it. You know, having no wife and all. They started to work the boat with Rex full time after they done dropped out."

"Did Rex Thompson have any interaction with Don Nguyen? Did they know each other?" Necaise asked, looking at his notes.

"They knew each other; all shrimpers do. But it was weird. Like they never talked, they just avoided each other. It was like they had together something nobody else did. Some folk says they had a past if you know what I mean."

Agent Necaise shook his head.

"At first, I took that Rex just didn't like the Vietnamese. You know there's folk 'round here who resent them coming over after the war and taking their jobs. You know the whole Viet family gets together to work a boat and get shrimp to market." Morley leaned forward in his chair and lowered his voice. "They can do this cheaper than us Americans. Pisses some locals off, if you know what I mean. I ain't no racist myself. I like them; they work hard and are generally good people. But some folk, you know are . . ."

"No, I don't know," Necaise said.

"Well, I don't judge Thompson just hated the Vietnamese. There's something else. Nobody could put their finger on it. They just avoided each other."

"Rex Thompson left town, what—about nine months ago? Have you seen him since, or do you know why he left?"

"Nope."

"Do you know where he went?"

"I ain't heard where he gone. Nobody knows. I tell you why he left, money. He was in deep shit up to his ears. Someone at the bank said to me he took a big loan out on his boat and pulled out the cash value. I'm sure he lost it all at the *boats*. You know when they brought them gambling riverboats to the Coast last year."

"Mr. Thompson was a gambler?"

"Sure, he just got sucked in. That's where his money's gone—card tables and booze," Morley said. "That's why he left. Why he lost the boat."

"His sons?"

"They tried to work the *Chasin' Tail* for the past few years and were really tore up when the bank took it. Made a lot of noise around town. They had their own problems, but I guess they could have kept the boat if their daddy hadn't pissed away all their money. Don Nguyen picked the boat up from the bank. I heard tell he didn't want it at first. The bank was selling it cheap, just to get some of their money back, you know. They kept lowering the asking price. Don didn't want it. He had four other boats." Morley shifted himself around in his big executive office chair.

Necaise thought the chair looked out of place in the harbormaster's otherwise sparse office with its dusty vinyl blinds. Watching Morley shift reminded him of how hard his wooden chair was. He wondered how Miss Gerard ever sat in one for hours grading homework.

Morley said, "Finally, his daughter Anh was getting married to Timmy Truong—you met them?"

"Yes, a nice couple."

"Don wanted to do something special, you know, for his daughter and new husband. Timmy wanted to learn to shrimp. So, a few months past, Don finally gave in and bought the boat from the bank. He had just renamed it the *Miss Anh* and was fixing to make ready for Timmy when it sank."

Necaise sat up in his chair and dropped his leg. "Any reason Timmy Truong might want to see the boat scuttled that you know?"

"No, Timmy was thrilled to have a boat. He is a great guy and loves Anh's family and has a lot of respect for Mr. Don. No, no way, Timmy would want that."

"Timmy, Jake, and Pigeon ever have any problems between them?" Necaise asked.

"Not that I know of. They knew each other but kept their distance, just like Don, and their daddy did."

A shrimping trawler coming into Back Bay passed under the raised highway drawbridge. Necaise had a splendid view of the boat, highlighted by the late afternoon sun. The outrigger towers stood straight up with the nets and tackle securely stowed on deck. The vessel was sitting low in the water, undoubtedly with tens of thousands of pounds of shrimp and ice in its hold. Car traffic backed up on either end of the drawbridge, and drivers waited. Just part of living on the Coast, he thought. Just the way it has always been.

"You find those peckers who sank it," Morley said.

Fred Necaise looked back at him and nodded.

CHAPTER 12

September 5, 1993

"*Con*, sit here. We can talk." Linh motioned to a cast iron bench under a large southern live oak in a grassy lot. Years ago, someone had placed the bench under the tree. It wasn't a park, just a vacant lot nobody claimed. Neighbors took turns mowing the grass and picking up litter. The bench, the tree, concrete steps to where a house had once been, and a rusted chain-linked fence were all that remained on the property.

Anh and Linh had just walked up a short hill after Sunday Mass at St. Michael Catholic Church. Each week, Linh attended the service to offer her prayers. She delighted in the round sanctuary, watching the rising sun dance off the tall vertical stained-glass windows. A small Vietnamese church just around the corner from their house conducted a service in her native language, but Linh preferred St. Michael's. She wanted to be able to pray in English. America was her new home. St. Michael's was her church.

"Sit, Thi Anh," Linh repeated, wiping off the bench for her. "I have something to talk to you about."

The massive oak shaded the two ladies from the bright sun. A gray squirrel hopped among the wild grasses and weeds in front of them, looking for nuts. Conical-shaped bald cypress trees across the street stood like sentinels along the sidewalk. In two months, they would turn brown and drop their needles.

"Did your father ever talk about the war with you?" Linh asked.

"No, not to me," Anh said.

"I didn't think so. This was very painful for him. When we left Quang Ngai, you were just four—you probably don't remember—we planned to leave our country for good. We left behind the things and memories that needed to stay. You are lucky you were too young to remember." Linh brushed a leaf off her white skirt, which had fallen from the branches above. "Your father suffered in the war. He suffered much."

Anh felt a warm breeze flutter the ruffles of her taffeta dress as she sat next to her mother. Her dress was the color of steamed milk. Anh gazed across the field to where two red birds were engaged in a fight with each other. One bird would hop up on its wings and dart towards the other, never making contact. The other bird would do the same. Again and again, the red birds sparred over something essential and known only to them.

"Did he ever mention to you the things we left behind?" Linh asked.

Anh shook her head.

"Bad things happened to your father during the war. He was an officer and had graduated from military college. At first, he worked in the South near Saigon. Like your grandfather, who was also an officer in the army but died early in the war, he was brilliant and smart. Your father spoke English well then. After we married, he worked with the American troops in Da Nang. He was the liaison officer. Do you understand what I mean?"

"Sort of," Anh answered, still looking at the red birds' fight.

"Before you were born, some money was stolen from a safe in Da Nang. It was money that belonged to the South Vietnamese government. Your father knew who stole the money and felt responsible for its theft. It was an American who did it. Your father's commanders concluded he should have done more to protect the money. They punished him and set an example for others." Linh placed her white-gloved hand on Anh's knee. "They took his job away and sent him on a dangerous mission in the jungle to fight the North Vietnamese."

The red birds seemed to have resolved their conflict and flew off to the cypress trees across the street. Anh and her mother were alone on the bench under the oak tree; nobody passed on the sidewalk in front.

"The enemy ambushed your father's platoon in the jungle. All his men died, and they took him prisoner and sent him to a prison camp. It was horrible for him there. They didn't kill him because he spoke English, and they assumed he might be in army intelligence. The North Vietnamese tortured him for nearly a year until he could escape. Had he told you any of this?"

"No, Mother; he said none of this to me." Anh was not sure she wanted to hear more.

Linh continued, "When he got back to the South, his commanders sent him to me. You were an infant, and he had not yet met you. We traveled to the coast and stayed with his aunt. She had a house on the beach where his uncle used to fish. I tried to make it *good* for your father. It was hard. Auntie took care of you, day and night, to give your father rest. I cooked all his favorite foods—*mì Quảng, bún chả cá* with fried fishcake, and *bún bò Huế*—and submitted myself as a wife should. I think I helped him. But he was a broken man. After two weeks, he was sent back to the war. They needed him."

A car with two young ladies in the front seat passed on the street. They tooted its horn. Anh looked up, lifted her left hand, and made a subtle wave of recognition. Linh pulled a white handkerchief out of her pocketbook and dabbed her eyes and forehead.

"Your father had an important job in Da Nang. The American who stole the money from the safe stole dignity from him as well. The suffering your father endured at the hands of the North would never have happened if he were not forced to take the blame for the theft. He often said he wished he had died with his men in the jungle rather than being taken, prisoner. Dealing with this challenged your father for many years. I could only hope to understand his torment. He suffered long after the war."

Anh turned to look at her mother. In her mother's eyes, she saw deep pain, more pain on her face than she ever saw before the drowning. It was as if her father's suffering—anguish and pain that she had always recognized in him but never understood—had transferred to her mother when he died. But Anh also saw passion and forgiveness in her eyes.

Linh said, "A few years after we came here to live, your father saw the American who had stolen the money in Da Nang. They recognized each other but never spoke. Your father's pain, which had settled down here, came back at once. It ate at his soul." Linh looked at her daughter and wondered if she could understand what her father had experienced. "I begged him to forget what had happened and forgive the man who caused him such pain. But he couldn't. Eventually, he tried to talk to this man. He was a shrimper. He saw him all the time. But he never could talk to him about the war."

Anh and Linh sat for a moment. Only the sounds of distant car traffic and wind in the tree filled the air.

"In his heart, though, I believe he forgave him. But he never told the man that or what he had endured. Your father never let him learn that he took the blame for the lost money and suffered at the hands of the North Vietnamese. He wanted to but couldn't," Linh said.

The red birds were back—at least Anh assumed they were the same birds—eating and pecking at the grass in front of the bench as if they had never fought.

"Did Father ever tell anyone but you about what had happened in the war?" Anh asked.

"No, not that I know of; nobody knew. He kept this to himself, and it destroyed him."

"Who was it that Father saw here?"

"Mr. Rex Thompson. Do you know of him?"

"No."

"I can't imagine you would. He has two sons, Jake and Peter. Did you see them at school? They're near your age."

"No, Mother," Anh said. "Do you forgive him, Mr. Thompson, I mean?"

"I forgave him years ago. But now I don't know what to think. You know your father bought the *Miss Anh* from the bank. But Mr. Thompson had owned the boat for many years before. I don't want to consider he had anything to do with your father's drowning, but I just can't release this from my mind."

"If he was involved, could you still forgive him?"

"I don't know if I can."

Anh twisted on the bench and grasped both of her mother's hands with hers. She looked into her mother's eyes to speak, but her words failed her, and she remained silent.

Two blocks away, the bells of St. Michael's started to ring. The last service of the day was ending. Soon, parishioners walking back up the gentle hill to their homes would greet them. It was time to dry their eyes and go as well.

• • •

He considered Jake and Pigeon the most obvious suspects. Necaise sat at his desk, leaned back in his chair, and looked up at the popcorn texture on the ceiling. A squat lamp with a green shade lit up files scattered across his desktop.

"Hey, Sidney," Necaise said, still studying the little white bumps. "You think the boys did it?" Sidney Catchot was the assistant district investigator who shared the office with Necaise.

"Sure, I think so." Sidney glanced up from his nearby desk.

"You rule out the father yet?" Necaise asked, still looking up at the ceiling. "Did you call Scranton?"

"Yeah, I don't think Rex had anything to do with this one. He was there, worked at a restaurant called The Crystal Chicken or something like that, a fried chicken joint. Some kind of local Scranton chain."

"How'd you find him, again?"

"Employment records. He wasn't hiding."

"Right."

"The owners were real nice and said he was there for about six months, then left sometime over the summer. They said they were sorry to see him go. It didn't sound like the same Rex Thompson folk around here knew. They said he was upfront about his time in Biloxi and his problems with booze. When he wasn't working, they told me he stayed at a place around the corner called the Lifeguard Mission."

"A church?" Necaise asked.

"Yeah, a church, as in 'My lifeguard walks on water' church. He found God there. Pastor Emanuel runs the place and serves, you know, the *down-and-out* crowd. Rex was a regular. Hard to believe."

Necaise grabbed his coffee mug and propped his heels on the edge of his desk.

"Rex pitched in to clean the kitchen and serve food. He never missed a talk or prayer service. The pastor didn't think he was ever gone long enough in August to slip down to Biloxi and back."

"You said the chicken place told you he worked for only six months? So, he wasn't there when the boat sank?"

"No, he wasn't there then. But he was still at the mission and had a cot there the entire time," Sidney tried to explain.

"But this Pastor Ezekiel—"

"Emanuel."

"He doesn't keep records of who is coming and going in his little prayer groups, does he?" Necaise asked.

"No, he just doesn't recall Rex gone during August. Now, about a week ago, Rex skipped out, and nobody at the mission has seen him since. Didn't tell nobody he was leaving, just left without saying a word. Real odd, they thought. Told nobody."

"Any idea where he went?" Necaise was now looking out the window.

Sidney shook his head but did not say a word, forcing Necaise to glance in his direction.

"Remember that incident back in '83 when those three Vietnamese got into a dustup with a few Biloxi oystermen?" Necaise asked.

"Yeah."

"Tensions were pretty high then, remember? Wasn't Thompson somehow involved in that fight?"

"No, I think he just saw it," Sidney said. "He was down at Gollott's when that guy Minor got in the face of those Vietnamese for dumping shells into the channel. Rex was one who saw the Viets climb on Minor's boat and exchange a few punches. That scuffle had nothing to do with Don Nguyen. He wasn't involved at all. They was oystermen."

"What about that time a few years back when those nets were cut on the *Mary Vu*? Wasn't Thompson a suspect then?" Necaise asked.

"No, not Rex. His sons were, though. In fact, they were the prime suspects."

"Convicted?"

"Nah. The Biloxi PD never could pin it on them. I'm sure they did it, though. Those boys never hid their hatred of the Vietnamese taking shrimp," Sidney said.

"Thompson boys could do it, sink the *Miss Anh*. No question?"

"In a heartbeat."

"How about those numbnuts who fired shots at that Viet boat out in the Gulf?" Necaise asked.

"Yeah, several years back. Not Nguyen. He never got caught up in all that shit. He was too even-tempered. I'm not aware he had any enemies here in Biloxi at all. Now, six years ago, there was a fire on one of his boats."

"What was the name?'

"The *Tien Hai*."

"Yeah, that's it."

"It looked like a firebombing, but the police never charged no one with the crime. They wrote it off as an accident. Nguyen insisted it was."

"That don't make sense," Necaise said.

"I told ya Nguyen was not looking for problems. Too smart for that."

"Okay, let's say the boys sank the *Miss Anh*. Why do you think they did it?"

"Because they're lowlifes," Sidney said.

"I don't doubt that, but there has got to be more to it. I think they couldn't stand the thought of them losing the boat to the bank. They probably thought Nguyen had something to do with it."

"They sank it out of spite?"

"Yeah, I think so. But there may be more. Last week after I met with Mrs. Nguyen, Timmy told me privately that his mother-in-law had more to say about Thompson but wasn't ready. He mentioned that Don and Rex might have had a history together, going back to the war. Timmy knew nothing else," Necaise said.

"Could the boys have been settling an old row between Don and their father?"

"Possible. The harbormaster also thought something was odd between the two."

"Think you should go talk to the brothers again, push them for an alibi?"

"No, that would only make them clam up. I bet they'll talk soon. You wait," Necaise said. "One of them will admit it to somebody. I suspect they sank the boat to get revenge. *Revenge always favors company*. They'll talk."

CHAPTER 13

September 15, 1993

Rex Thompson opened his eyes when the Greyhound rumbled over the steel grating at the top of the Back Bay Bridge. He looked out the bus window, over the water to the City of Biloxi. After three days of travel, he stank; his clothes were filthy; he needed a shave, but he was home.

It had been nine months since Rex left the Coast. He fled when he had no reason to stay. Now, he was not sure why he was coming back.

The bus stopped with a hiss of air brakes at the small Biloxi terminal. Rex pulled himself out of his seat and stiffly made his way down the aisle and off the bus. Other passengers turned at once to retrieve their belongings from the luggage hold; Rex had none. He shuffled out to the street.

Gray stubble softened the edges of his sharp jawline and sunken cheeks. Weathered wrinkles radiated, like spokes of a tire, from the outer corners of his eyes. His hair, which was once a proud jet black, hung about his ears and collar in greasy, gray curls. Rex wore a faded flannel coat over dirty black canvas pants. His disheveled appearance and slow, stiff hobble spoke "homelessness." Other pedestrians on the sidewalk gave him space.

He made his way over the railroad tracks and down to the Jubilee

Worship Mission Church, where he remembered he could get a hot meal. He had eaten nothing since Memphis.

• • •

The Ford Ranger came down the drive and pulled up in front of the house. "Dad's back," Pigeon said from the open driver's side window.

Jake was sitting on the front steps, flipping through a magazine on guns and ammo. He looked up to see Pigeon behind the wheel. Amber and her boyfriend sat next to him on the bench seat with their arms around each other.

"So," Jake mumbled.

"So? He's our dad. I heard he's been walking around for two days. Thought ya want to know."

Jake studied an advertisement in the magazine, then ripped out the page, folded it, and stuffed it into his shirt pocket. "So, he up and leaves us like crap, no explanation, nothing, and you want me to git all excited about him coming back?"

"Whatever, asshole. Why are you jerking me?"

"Pigeon, we need to talk," Jake said, "later." He motioned to Amber and her boyfriend. "Need to talk."

"I don't give a shit what ya think. I'm going git 'im, bring him home. He can have my bed. I'll take the couch."

"Don't do it."

Jake watched Amber flame a glass bowl with a small butane torch. She inhaled the fumes then passed the *pookie* to her boyfriend, who did the same. White smoke swirled out the open windows of the truck as Amber tossed the pipe and torch onto the dash. She then arched her head back while her boyfriend kissed her neck and slid his hand over her shoulder and down the front of her shirt.

"You ain't bitching me, Jake," Pigeon said with his hands firmly gripping the steering wheel.

"Not bitching you. We need to be smart about this, think shit through, ya know," Jake said.

"I'll do what I damn want."

Pigeon then turned the truck around in the clearing. Without saying a word, Amber's boyfriend stuck his free hand—the one he didn't have on her breast—out the window and flipped his middle finger at Jake. The Ranger then sped down the drive, spinning a cloud of dust.

• • •

Morning sunlight filtered through the dirty kitchen window. Jake and his father sat at the dinette, looking at each other but not speaking. The smell of strong coffee and chicory filled the room.

"How're ya gittin along?" Rex eventually asked, then took a sip of coffee.

"We're fine." Jake looked up from the table and noticed someone had opened the yellow curtains.

"Pigeon says that y'all are working down at the Anderson place."

"Just doing some cleanup, ya know."

"Making enough for groceries, I see. Thanks for the grub. I'm fixing to work and pay you back for breakfast."

"Shit, what you going to do? All ya know's shrimping and boozing."

"I'll git work. Figure I'll go looking tomorrow," Rex said. "I'm surprised you still have this dump." Rex pushed his dirty plate aside, cupped both hands around the warm coffee, and glanced around the room.

"Nobody asked for your got-damn opinion. Listen, Dad cut the crap. You owe us an explanation. You can't just bounce out when the shit hits. It's been hell here since ya left. Hell, it was hell here before ya left. You didn't make it any better when you rolled. You left us in a shithole." Jake scooted his metal chair backward, stood, and got a Coke from the icebox.

"I'm sorry. I have no excuse." Rex said.

"Sorry, doesn't cut shit. What'd ya expect us to do after you cashed out?"

"I know. Sorry is a piss ant's way of covering up my failure. Jake, I left because I had to. I bummed to Pennsylvania—rolling hills, Liberty Bell, you know. I got as far as Scranton and just stopped. No reason. I had no money and—"

"We had no fucking money."

"I know. I said, sorry. I'm just trying to explain and maybe someday git things right with you and Pigeon. Up North, I went dry. I stopped and hadn't had one since. Stone-cold sober. But being sober don't go far when you ain't got no job, no money, no place to stay, and nothing to eat. I worked a kitchen awhile. The owners were nice folk. No gambling boats in Pennsylvania. I made some dough, got by."

"So, you show up here broke. Where's your cash?"

Rex did not answer.

"Your story is so full of shit. This dog don't hunt, man."

Pigeon opened the bathroom door and plodded into the living room, naked except for a towel wrapped around his waist.

Jake turned to his brother. "Jesus, go put some damn clothes on. Man, ain't nobody here want to see your balls."

Ignoring him, Pigeon walked over to the counter and poured a cup of coffee. He looked at Jake. "Top of the morning to you, too, ya little shit." He then said to his father, "How are y'all doing? Getting reacquainted and all?"

"Sure, I'm just telling Jake what I told you last night."

Pigeon pulled up another chair and sat at the dinette, holding the warm mug with both hands. "Tell Mr. Prick here how ya gave all your money from washing dishes to the church in Scranton. Go on. Tell 'im."

"Back off, Pigeon," Rex said.

"Just trying to git all the shit out on the table, Dad."

"Okay, I did," Rex said. "I gave what I earned to the mission where I stayed at."

"I can't believe this shit. Gave all your money to a got-damn church?" Jake asked.

"That's right. I found Jesus."

Jake looked at Pigeon and then to his father sitting across the table. Great, Jake thought, I've got Captain Flasher for a brother and a Jesus freak for a father. "Praise the Lord. God, help me. You didn't come here to preach our asses, did ya?"

"No, of course not. I'm not sure why I came home. I'm hoping to know someday," Rex said.

"Jake, go easy. Dad's not trippin' on you, man. Give 'im some space." Pigeon half-stood and adjusted the towel that was coming loose around his waist.

"I guess one reason I came back was to ask y'all's forgiveness." Rex set his coffee cup aside and put his hands together on the table. "I've not been the best of fathers. I could've done better. But I've always loved you."

Jake stood, threw his empty can in the sink, and pushed open the front door. "I can't take this shit anymore. You and Pretty Boy just knock yourselves out. I'm gittin some air."

"Jake, sit the fuck down," Rex said, slamming his fists on the table. "I'm not done talking. Not perfect, never been. I'm trying."

"Dad, you should've stayed gone. Pige and I don't want you here no more."

"That's not true," Pigeon shot back.

Jake let the screen slam home behind him without looking back. A gentle breeze coming off the bay smelled of sulfur and rotten eggs. Jake recognized the odor of decaying vegetation along the exposed shoreline during extreme low tide. Fitting, he thought, his life stank—why not the goddamn air he breathed, too? Jake stepped around the house and walked down a path toward the water's edge, where he could think things through.

Their father's return complicated their situation. He and Pigeon sank the *Miss Anh* because they couldn't stand the idea of someone else having the boat. He didn't know Timmy, Anh, or Don at all. He didn't care to. At the time, he hadn't heard one fricking word from their father in eight months. Their dad could have been dead, just as likely as lying in a gutter with vomit and piss. Yeah, he was mad at his father, mad that he raised him and his brother in such a hellhole and then left.

It wasn't right that the bank took the boat. It pissed him off that the Vietnamese eventually got it. The Viets got everything they could get their grubby hands on. Maybe it was revenge.

Jake stepped over the skiff and climbed up to a narrow wooden dock. The pier extended over the mud flats for about twenty feet. During low tide, it did not reach the water's edge. He sat at the end where the seagulls had not yet littered the deck with white droppings.

The drowning, Jake thought, shouldn't have happened. Don should have been able to get off the boat like Timmy. *Damn, this fucks the whole thing up.* Now his father was back—full of the Lord, sober, but broke—who knows what he'll think when he eventually finds out he and Pigeon sank the boat? Jake thought he knew his dad before when he was a drunkard. Now his dad seemed to be a stranger to him.

A brown pelican with its wings tucked back and mouth wide open plunged thirty feet from the sky into a splash of muddy water. The bird popped up like a cork and gulped its catch down its thin neck. The pelican aired its feathers before climbing out of the water with webbed feet and broad, flapping wings until airborne. Jake watched the bird glide out over the bay and out of sight.

CHAPTER 14

September 20, 1993 - Morning

Early the following day, Rex left the house to look for work. A thunderstorm had passed during the night, and the trees still dripped on the shell drive. Wet brush at the edge of the muddy tire tracks forced Rex to pick his way down the soggy center strip.

The scent of rain on leaves always stirred memories of his youth—memories of time complicated in a different way. As he walked, Rex's mind wandered to Galveston, to his childhood. He thought about the time when he was five or six and dressed as a ghost for Halloween. A white sheet, with holes cut out for his eyes, covered him to his ankles. He carried a paper candy sack, painted orange to look like a pumpkin. Evelyn, his older sister, was dressed as a witch and had a pillowcase from their mother's linen closet to collect her treats. She worked a stick of gum between her teeth.

As he and his sister canvassed the neighborhood for goodies, the sheet kept sliding around on his face, making it difficult for him to see. To fix the problem, Evelyn took the gum from her mouth, stuck it to the top of his head, and smashed the sheet down to hold it in place.

At the far end of the neighborhood, it started to rain. Brother and sister ran for home. He held his sheet to his face with one hand, and with the other, his wet paper sack. The bottom of the bag eventually collapsed, and the candy scattered across the street. They stopped to salvage his loot, collecting it in Evelyn's pillowcase.

He recalled the sweet, musky odor of wet leaves in the road and gutters that night. Rex touched the top of his head and ran his fingers through his short-cropped hair to feel the spot where his sister's gum got stuck, and his mother had to cut it out with her shears. Yesterday, he visited a barber for a haircut and a shave and washed his clothes at the Duds-n-Suds. Rex was now trying to stay clean, dry, and presentable as he tiptoed through the wet grass between the tire tracks.

• • •

"Rex, what a surprise," the floor manager said. "I can't believe it."

"In-person," Rex replied.

"Come in. Where've you been? Haven't seen you in months. Come in. Sit down." Matt Gautier beckoned him through the door and into the corner office of the car dealership. Matt didn't bother to get up from his big chair or offer his hand. Beads of sweat made Matt's pie-shaped face glisten in the showroom's bright fluorescent light coming in through a glass wall.

Rex thought Matt looked like he had fattened up since he had last seen him. With Spanner Ford embroidered above the pocket, his red polo shirt was unbuttoned entirely at the collar to accommodate his thick neck.

"Where've you been?" Matt asked.

"Up north, Pennsylvania. Been there?"

"Nope. Hey, go ahead, sit."

Rex eased into a chair with faux burgundy leather and dark wooden legs. Matt sat behind a matching fake wood desk. Rex judged the office furniture choice to be a lame effort to impress potential car buyers with a show of style and taste. "You look like you're doing okay here. Your lot looks full of new ones."

"I'm doing mighty fine, Rex. What brings you back? What can I do for you?"

"I'm trying to git right with myself and my boys. Not drinking no more. Been sober as a judge, nine months."

"Good for you."

"Matt, you know we go back. Never asked you for nothing in the past. But right now, I need a favor, need a job."

"Sure."

"I'll do anything. I just need a little cash to git me started. Made some mistakes lately, and I'm just a little short."

"Sure, Rex, I can find you something here. I'll set you up in the shop. In a minute, go around back, talk to Mikey. I'll let 'im know you're coming." Matt lifted the receiver and pushed intercom buttons. "I can only start you off at minimum. I've kids working for that, and I can't pay more. Mikey will get you set up."

"Anything. Appreciate it, Matt." Rex started to stand.

"Sorry to hear about the boat. Tragic what happened to Don Nguyen; the family is all tore up, I hear," Matt said while waiting for Mikey to pick up the line.

"What boat?"

"Your old boat, the *Chasin' Tail*."

"What?"

"Yeah, Don Nguyen scarfed it up from the bank, June or July, I don't know. Someone scuttled it in the bay last month. Don drowned."

Rex felt his throat thicken. His eyes darted around the room until they fixed on a faded photo on the wall of Matt, years younger and a hundred pounds lighter, standing on the back of a fishing boat and holding a cobia that was at least forty inches long. A teenage boy—it must be his son—was standing behind him with a big smile and doing a double thumbs-up. The tightness in Rex's throat intensified. He could feel his temples throb. He couldn't swallow or speak.

"Rex, you okay?"

Rex nodded and sat back in the fake leather chair. He hadn't heard of the boat sinking or the drowning before this moment, but he knew he was somehow involved.

Rex squeaked out a reply, "I was gone. I didn't know. What happened?"

Matt put down the receiver and told him what was in the news, all the facts. But he didn't tell Rex the rumors, the shop talk in the back, the speculations on who did it, the stories about motives and revenge, or his guess that Jake and Pigeon committed the crime.

Rex felt ill and needed air. An awkward moment passed. "Can I start tomorrow?"

"Sure, Rex. Seven?"

Rex nodded.

Matt watched his friend, and one-time drinking buddy, shuffle out through sleek new cars in the bright showroom.

Rex, his head spinning, stopped at a fire-engine red 5.0 LX Mustang convertible with its top dropped. He put his hand on top of the windshield frame and leaned over: actual black leather bucket seats, five-speed manual transmission, two hundred horsepower—a real muscle pony. For a moment, Rex dreamed of another time and place to be. He then stiffened and turned for the door.

• • •

Once more, he smelled the musky scent of wet leaves when he reached the long driveway to the house. The grass on the median was now dry, but the woods on either side remained wet. Rex saw himself again as a kid with Evelyn on their porch. The rain was making a racket above on the tin roof, then running off the edge in sheets. Evelyn had dumped her pillowcase full of their joint loot on the gray painted wood. Rex sat with his older sister counting Chicklets, Hot Tamales, Turkish Taffy, Dots, and Necco Wafers. The act of reclaiming their candy was underway. Counting, separating, negotiating, and sharing the trove of sweets consumed them—the artificial fruity candy scent mixed with the musk of wet leaves.

When Rex finally stepped into the camp, Jake and Pigeon were gone. Dirty dishes littered the kitchen. He stepped to the icebox and pulled out two cans of beer. Rex slouched across the room, sat on the sagging couch, and placed the beer on the coffee table in front of him.

Staring at the beer cans, Rex worried about what Matt had just told him. He knew right away that Jake and Pigeon had sunk the boat. It was something he knew they could do. Stupid. He might have done the same at their age. Did he raise them to be like himself?

For the first time in years, Rex started to think about *his* father. He struggled to piece together a happy memory of him. Time spent with his father was rare and often clouded with conflict. The last time he ever saw his father was a few months after being dressed as a Halloween ghost; it was the night the police came to the house.

Yelling, screaming, and the shattering of dishes in the kitchen had awakened Rex and his sister. Mother was crying. Shouting. The dog was barking.

Evelyn got out of bed and cracked the bedroom door. A sliver of light streamed into the room. Rex dropped from his mattress and slid under the bed. Evelyn closed the door and crawled next to him.

The dog snarled. Rex heard the kitchen door slam open against a wall. The dog gave out a loud, pained yelp as if being kicked in the gut. A gun fired. The barking stopped. Evelyn and Rex held each other tight. Rex started to cry.

The room suddenly flooded with light. Rex saw a silhouette of his father standing in the doorway, a bottle in one hand and a gun in the other.

Mother grabbed at the gun. He pushed her off.

"No," she pleaded, "leave 'em alone."

"Where's the got-damn bastard children?" their father yelled. He stumbled into the room and fell to the wooden floor. His face landed just inches from Evelyn's, and she gasped. Their father flicked the empty bottle across the floor and grabbed Evelyn by her hair.

"Here's my swee' little girl," he slurred, then pulled Evelyn out from under the bed.

"No, Daddy."

"Who ya like more, me or ya mamma?"

Evelyn struggled against his grip and screamed when she saw the steel-blue of the pistol in his hand. He aimed the gun at Mother's chest. Mother froze in the doorway.

"Who ya love more, dammit?" he yelled at Evelyn again.

Rex buried his face in his hands.

Mother screamed.

"Mother, shut up, ya bitch!" their father yelled.

Rex's eyes popped opened when the sound of a gunshot exploded in the room. Glass shattered on the floor below the bedroom window. Mother collapsed in the doorway.

"Please. Please leave us alone. Leave now. Please leave," Mother pleaded.

Rex's father let go of Evelyn, and she scrambled to her mother's arms. His father got to his knees, placing the muzzle of the Smith & Wesson .38 Special against the side of his head. Rex heard the hammer set.

"You're all fucking bitches. I hate you."

"Wayne!" Mother yelled.

Another gunshot.

From under the bed, young Rex could see his father kneeling in the center of the room. He had a dazed and disconnected look in his eyes. White dust drifted down from the ceiling above and settled on his shoulders and dark-brown hair.

The sound of approaching sirens then cut through the night air. Mother sobbed. Blue lights flashed in the broken window.

"It's all fucked up." Rex's father said. He dropped the revolver on the floor, stood, and left the room.

That was the last time Rex ever saw him.

Rex's thoughts returned to his sons and the boat. He looked at the beer cans in front of him; beads of condensation ran down their sides in rivulets. The liquid pooled on the coffee table around the bottom of the unopened cans. Rex put his hands to his face and wept.

CHAPTER 15

September 20, 1993 - Evening

He jerked open the screen and pushed the front door in with his knee. It was dusk. Gnats had attacked the back of his neck and ankles, and he could no longer sit on the steps and read.

"What you got there?" Jake asked from where he lay on the sofa.

"The New Testament." Rex held out a small green paperback book as he entered the room.

"Bible?"

"Yeah, part of it."

"Shit, you're really gone loco."

"I've come a long way, Jake."

"What does it say about fucking your life over with booze? Or putting your sons' rightful inheritance on the poker table, huh? What does it say about that shit?" Jake propped his head on his elbow and glared at his dad.

"Don't test me."

"I fucking will if I want."

"It says to forgive and seek forgiveness. That's what it says."

"Shit." Jake reclined on the couch and looked across the room to a credenza where a television once sat. "You believe that shit?"

"Where's Pigeon?" Rex asked.

"Out."

"I want to talk to you boys when he gits back, both y'all." Rex stepped into the hallway.

"About what?"

"Something."

"Listen, Dad, I'm trying to git cool with the idea of you coming back and all. Can't just come at us all heavy and shit. Okay?" Jake said.

"I understand. Y'all need space. I'm good with that. Let me know when he comes in." Rex shut the bedroom door behind him and flicked on the light.

• • •

"Pige's here," Jake said with a rap on the door.

It was two o'clock in the morning, and Jake and Pigeon had been working things out on the front steps for over an hour. They would deny any involvement with the sinking of the *Miss Anh*. They knew nothing about it; a real shock when they read the papers; couldn't imagine anyone would do such a thing; a real shame the old guy drowned; should have been a better swimmer if you wanted to shrimp. They rehearsed their story: dinner at about six, watched some TV, ran over to the BP Station to get more beer at about eleven, listened to Led Zeppelin and Aerosmith, Pigeon fell asleep on the couch, Jake slept in the back bedroom, got up about nine, went to Burger Barn for breakfast and heard for the first time about the boat. They had planned out some of the stories before the sinking; the rest they had made up tonight. Their alibis were tight—nothing to worry about.

Rex stepped out of the bedroom, wearing a green camo sweat suit he had borrowed from Jake. Pigeon paced the room from the kitchen to the credenza. Jake sank into the sofa and put his bare feet on the coffee table.

"You got it, Dad. We're listening," Jake said. "Go for it."

Rex pulled up a chair facing the sofa where he could look at both of his sons. "I heard the boat sank last month."

"Yeah, real shocker, man," Jake said.

"Matt, down at the Ford place, told me. I went looking for a job. I saw right off you boys were somehow—"

"Bullshit, we don't know what the hell you're talking about."

Pigeon nodded his head in agreement.

"I guess I'm surprised the cops haven't arrested y'all," Rex said.

"Shit, we had nothing to do with it. That night, we was here—the whole damn night. We was drinking some brews and listening to Aerosmith. Watched TV before it broke, ya know, *Home Improvement*. Ya know, Tim Allen."

Pigeon piped in, "They's got us on video at BP."

"Listen, Dad. We had jack shit to do with that boat. Nada," Jake said. "I hope they catch the bastards who done it."

"Hey, I'm not trying to pass judgment. If y'all are messed up in this thing, I want to help."

"No help needed, Pops, 'cus we's clean," Jake said. "Got it?"

Rex had heard enough. Perhaps his sons were telling the truth. His gut told him otherwise. He wasn't some private detective, he thought. What duty to the public—or God for that matter—did he have to speculate, stick his nose around? But his past connected him to Don Nguyen more than most people, including his own two sons, knew. This he could not change.

It bothered him that he never got the chance to talk to Don since they first met again at the boatyard. They seemed like opposing magnets, never able to get close enough to speak. Rex had sensed Don had a thing to tell, something to get off his chest, but never did. It satisfied Rex over the years to ignore the past. But now that Don was dead, unanswered questions peppered his mind

"Fine, I'll drop it. You don't need to tell me no more," Rex said and got up from the chair.

Pigeon, still pacing the room, said, "You're right about that Pops, 'cuz we don't know shit."

Rex returned to his room. He held his New Testament to his chest with both hands. He knew that sleep wouldn't come easy for him tonight.

• • •

"Jake Thompson got himself a handgun," Sidney said, busting into the field office with a printout from the FBI.

"How's that?" Necaise responded.

Sidney walked around Necaise's desk and showed him the paper. "No criminal record. No priors. Nothing says he can't."

"Any thought on why he might want one? Where did he get it?"

"Dollar Pawn on Lemoyne, last week, Ruger Security-Six .357 Magnum."

"Alright, tell the Biloxi PD. But I don't want no rookie cops spooking him. Leave the brothers alone; just keep tabs on them." Necaise said. "Okay?"

"Got it. I think the brothers are feeling the heat, you?"

"They got themselves in over their heads. I just hope they don't do nothing stupid."

"Think they'll run?" Sidney asked.

"No. Right now, we need to give the boys some space, let them think they got away with it."

"Sure thing, Boss Man," Sidney said. "I'm going to Nancy's for breakfast. Want something?"

"No."

Sidney left the office, looking at the printout.

Necaise reflected on what Timmy Truong had said to him a few weeks past that Mrs. Nguyen had "something to say." He thought those were the words used. Timmy had not contacted him recently, and Necaise wondered if he should call. The case was going nowhere. The prime suspects, Jake and Pigeon, had every reason to sink the boat. But nothing tangible connected them.

Necaise determined that the boat was sabotaged sometime between eleven at night and four o'clock in the morning when both Timmy and Don were sleeping. Timmy had been doing repair work on the deck all evening until he went to bed. He would have noticed anyone approach the boat.

Video from the BP gas station showed Jake and Pigeon walking into the store to buy a twelve-pack of Bud Lite just before eleven. Pigeon even smiled at the camera on the way out the door. A waitress at the Burger Barn remembered the brothers having breakfast the morning the boat sank. News spread fast in this small town, especially over morning coffee. According to the waitress, when a man approached the boys' booth to tell them that the *Chasin' Tail* had been sunk, Pigeon slapped the table and said something like, "No way, man." Jake then got up and paced around the floor, spouting off about how unfair it was that their old boat had been "scuttled." Scuttled was the word the waitress recalled. According to the waitress, the boys seemed overly dramatic in their response to the story, something she considered odd. Camera footage of the Burger Barn parking lot recorded the Ranger pulling in just after nine in the morning and leaving an hour later.

There was plenty of time between eleven and four to put a small outboard motor on the back of a johnboat, slip four miles out to Deer Island, attach a cable to the prop and anchor line of the *Miss Anh*, and return. Necaise had looked it up: there was no moon that night, and it was dark on the bay.

Sidney poked his head into the office two hours later while holding a fresh cup of coffee in one hand. "I just found out from the Department that Rex is back in town. He came in on a bus a few days ago and is staying at the house, working at Spanner Ford, odd jobs, and such."

"Interesting. Know why he's back?"

"No, just kind of showed up. Looks like he's trying to clean up his act. He visits the Jubilee Mission. Preacher, I understand, says he's helpful and all. He said Rex was *saved*."

"Think the boys called him back?"

"I can't see why. I don't think Rex is in on this," Sidney said.

"Yeah. Just complicates things for the boys, don't it?" Necaise made a mental note to drop in on the Jubilee Mission, talk to Rex, and see what side of the truth he was on.

CHAPTER 16

September 22, 1993

"*Cháu* Thi Anh, it so nice to see you," Pham Van Lu said while standing in his doorway. He extended his arm to open the screen. "Come in."

"*Chào Chú* Lu," Anh said with a subtle bow as she entered a small living area.

Lace curtains covered two tiny windows, rendering the room dim. On the bare wood floor, an arrangement of sparse furnishings appeared haphazard. No little knickknacks sat scattered about to collect dust. No pictures covered the walls. The home of a middle-aged bachelor, Anh thought.

"Please sit. I'm so sorry to hear about your father. I'm embarrassed I have not yet called on your mother to give condolence. Please forgive me, *Cháu*."

"Thank you. I'll tell my mother."

"I sent a card."

"Thank you, *Chú* Lu."

Lu waved Anh to sit in an upholstered chair with a soft, clean, white fabric that seemed out of place in the darkened room. Only guests use this chair, she thought.

Anh had known Lu almost her entire life and considered him an uncle, despite no actual family relation. She suspected he and her father had a great deal in common. She knew both men had been officers in the South Vietnamese Army during the war and fought many years against the Communists. But she knew little more about her father's history in the war and nothing else about Lu's life in Vietnam. Nobody ever talked of the war.

"What surprise. What bring you to my home this afternoon?"

"I have something I would like you to read for me, please," Anh said. She held out a small book, no larger than a deck of cards, with a tan, stained and worn, fabric binding. "I found this yesterday in a box of some of my father's things. It's written in Vietnamese. I'm hoping you can translate it for me. I think it's from the war."

"Does your mother know this book? Why didn't you ask her to read it?"

"It was hidden. I don't think she knows about it," Anh said.

"Why do you think?"

"She talked to me about Father and the war recently but never mentioned anything he might have brought with him from Vietnam. She doesn't know about the book."

"You certain?" Lu asked.

"Yes. This is something Father kept secret. I am sure. I need to find out why."

Lu took the book, sat in a brown, overstuffed recliner, and turned on a lamp over his shoulder. The yellow light cast a sharp shadow across his face and stressed the angularity of his features. In the glow, Anh noticed he had calloused hands, much like her father. Years of shucking oysters, picking shrimp, hauling boat lines, and mending nets had taken a toll on both men.

Lu said, "It look like a journal or maybe a memoir. It begin 'April 6th, 1972. Quang Tri Combat Base.' That's up north. 'I am Captain Nguyen Duc Dung, 1st Division, 1st Corps.' Do you want me read for you now?"

"Yes, please."

Lu read aloud while translating into English, "'It been two months since I have escaped from North Vietnamese prison camp in Laos. I have rejoined my unit. Soon I will be sent to Cam Lo River, defend our precious country against the ruthless and evil North Vietnamese enemy who is attacking home and trying to break spirit. I have story to tell, and I fear I must write it down now, or it will go to the grave with me soon.'" Lu looked up at Anh. "Your father describe what would call the Easter Offensive. None of us on front lines expect to go home."

Anh sat at the edge of the white chair and listened to her *uncle* read from the faded pages. With a soft, deep timbre in his voice, Lu read her father's story about how he grew up in a military family and was taught as a young boy to be patriotic and to love his country. Details of his early years in the war and his rapid climb to the rank of captain sang out in translation as if he wrote the words in poetic prose, despite Lu's broken English.

Dung wrote of his time at Bien Hoa and fighting the Vietcong during the Tet Offensive in 1968. He wrote of being introduced to Anh's mother in Quang Ngai by a mutual friend and how he fell in love. Their relationship blossomed with the exchange of letters while Dung served at the air base in Da Nang. Three months later, he returned to Quang Ngai to seek acceptance from Linh's family for marriage. Nguyen Duc Dung wed Hoang Thuy Linh the following day. The newlyweds had only hours together before Dung returned to Da Nang, leaving his bride in the care of his extended family. Dung was assigned to the Army Liaison Office for the US 366th Tactical Fighter Wing at the air base.

"'It honor me to be given most coveted job, a post that reflect my honesty, integrity, and loyalty to the cause of people of South Vietnam.'" Lu continued to translate.

"*Chú* Lu, help me with the places. Where is Da Nang and, you say, Bien Hoa?" Anh asked.

"Vietnam is shaped like dragon—climbing dragon—climbing up South China Sea." Lu made a long sweeping motion with his hand. "Head is north, and tail is south. The body was cut half in 1954 after the war between Communists in the North and French in the South. You were born in Quang Ngai, halfway up coast in the South."

"Like my parents?"

"Yes, me too. We were all born in Province Quang Ngai. Bien Hoa is about four hundred mile south of Quang Ngai, near the city of Saigon, which now called Ho Chi Minh City. Da Nang about ninety mile north of Quang Ngai, also along the coast. Now, Quang Tri and Cam Lo are hundred mile more north, next to what was border of North Vietnam. You know, 1975, the Communists defeated South and took all of Vietnam," Lu said.

Anh nodded.

"Let me continue. 'On December 13th, 1970, my world turned upside-down when I found Airman Rex Thompson steal thousands of dollars from the government South Vietnam. My error was to take airman for his speak and not arrest him. This mistake ruin my reputation and gave dishonor to my family.'"

The bits were coming together with what her mother had told her, Anh thought.

For many written pages, Dung described how he felt unjustly punished for not safeguarding the money and how angry he was that his command never discussed this matter with their American counterparts. Airman Thompson was never questioned about the theft, and Dung felt he most likely left the country with the money.

"'My command officer, Colonel Le Dinh Lao, wanted to destroy me for what I had done and set an example around my ranks. You see, theft brought embarrassment to Colonel Lao, and only by breaking me could he fix his reputation. I was not allowed court-martial to tell my story. As punishment, they sent me to jungles of Laos, where I sure to be meet the enemy.'"

Lu then asked, "Thi Anh, are sure you want me continue reading?"

"Yes, I need to know."

Lu resumed reading the words Anh's father had written when she was only a baby. "'Colonel Lao sent me to 1st Armored Brigade in 1st Division while it desperately try to leave Laos and return to Vietnam. The army was attempted to empty troops from a failed operation gone largely bad. When I joined the brigade, the enemy was already shelling our column from all directions.'"

Lu spoke, "Thi Anh, they call this Operation Lam Son 719, named after the village of Lam Son, the legend birthplace of Le Loi who defeated the invading Chinese in 1427. Le Loi is famous Vietnamese hero."

These details reminded Anh of how little she knew about the history of her native country.

"We went to Laos in 1971 to attack North Vietnamese Army, which was using this country to do their strikes on us. The Americans would not send troops to Laos because they say it was a neutral country. Neutral on paper, they say, yes. *Bullsheet*. . . . Excuse me, Anh." Lu continued to explain. "The Laotians allowed the North to run in their country with freedom."

Anh sensed that Lu still carried strong feelings of the war as her father must have had. "Please, read on."

On the pages, Dung described the remnants of an infantry company recently placed under his command. He wrote about how he often had to escort his men on patrols to scout enemy positions. When the armored brigade was just ten kilometers from the South Vietnamese border, they learned that two enemy regiments were waiting to ambush them along the road ahead.

The brigade commander, Colonel Luat, radioed for air support to clear the route. Airborne forces swept the enemy from the path ahead, but the word of this action never got back to the armored brigade. Without this information, the commander had no choice but to leave the road and head down jungle trails to look for an unguarded route home. It was then that the 1st Armored Brigade came to the steep banks of the Se Pone River and couldn't get their tanks and armored personnel carriers across to the safety of Vietnam.

"They were like resting ducks," Lu added. "Sitting, I mean. Pinned down with river on one side and the enemy on other side."

Dung then wrote that when the brigade stalled at the Se Pone River, his command ordered him to take a platoon beyond their defense perimeter and survey the enemy positions. It was on this mission that his small band of hand-picked infantry came under enemy fire. Bullets destroyed their radio, and they could not summon reinforcements or broadcast their position. Dung watched all his men die as enemy forces overwhelmed them. Dung survived the battle, and the North Vietnamese took him, prisoner.

"*Cháu*, I think I should stop and read this to myself first," Lu said.

"No."

The journal continued with a vivid description of Dung being hauled north along the Ho Chi Minh Trail in the rear of a truck, bound and gagged. During the first three days, his captors denied him food and water. For weeks at a time, they confined him in bamboo cages with his wrists tied behind his back. The enemy put a garotte around his neck and fastened it above his head in such a way it prevented him from sitting. Eventually, his captors sent him to a prison camp surrounded by a bamboo fence and punji sticks, deep within the jungles of Laos, where the torture began.

"I can't read this to you. I'm going to stop. Leave this with me, and I'll write later your father's words for you."

"Skip this part if you must, but please continue," Anh said.

Lu flipped forward through several pages and said, "Your father survived ten-month as prisoner of war, and then by grace of God, was able to escape and find his way home. Here is where he talk about seeing you for first time at his aunt house. 'I held her like a lotus flower in my palm. Her skin, like cream; her hair, like black lacquer; her little voice, like the coo of a dove. I felt real joy for first time in many month.'"

Tears leaked off the lower edge of Anh's eyes and down her cheeks. With the tip of her tongue, Anh tasted their saltiness at the corner of her mouth.

"He talk about your mother as well and how happy was his join with her. It would embarrass me to read to you right now." Lu read to himself for a few minutes then said, "*Trời ơi*. I can't believe . . ."

"What?" Anh asked.

"This cannot be true."

"Please, tell me what you see."

Lu flipped back a few pages. "Your father wrote, 'I was allowed to spending two weeks with my loving wife and my baby daughter and get my strength after suffering much with the North Vietnamese enemy. After, I was sent back to Hue City, to my company. It was there, in Hue, I learn that after my capture in Laos, the 1st Armored Brigade was saved from certain destroy by two bulldozers brought in by helicopter to cut path in steep bank of the Se Pone River.'

"This is part so alarming. Do you remember Colonel Lao, your father's commander in Da Nang, who sent him to Laos?" Lu asked.

"Yes, he wanted to make an example of Father."

"This is what your father wrote, 'I found out it was Colonel Lao who deliberately fail to tell Colonel Luat, the 1st Armored Brigade commander, that airborne cleared Route 9 and thrown out North Vietnamese forces. If Colonel Luat had known this, he never would have left the road for jungle trail and never gotten pinned at Se Pone River. I'm sure it was my presence in the 1st Armored Brigade that led Colonel Lao to withhold this information. I brought dishonor to self and embarrassed Colonel Lao in Da Nang. In Laos, he punish me more.' Your father thought it was because of him hundreds of his fellow soldiers died without necessary."

"He couldn't really believe this. Could he?" Anh asked.

"Yes, this is what your father would believe. In 1978, I met your father for first time here in Biloxi. I never knew him during war. We hardly talk about our experience there. But over years, I understand your father's character. He was a man of perfect honesty and integrity. He grabbed responsibility for every action. I am sure your father connected disgrace he brought to himself in Da Nang with action of Colonel Lao that put his fellow soldiers in harm's away. He was just that type of man."

"What happened to Colonel Lao?"

Lu scanned the last few pages of the journal. "Your father doesn't say. But Lam Son was big failure for us. It show the world South Vietnamese people did not have will to make army and government that could fight North Vietnam without America help. Many believe Lam Son 719 was reason American president Nixon decide war was not worth sacrifice of more American lives. If what your father say is true, that Colonel Lao harmed 1st Armored Brigade because of him, then your father assumed burden no man could hold. The result of war may have, they say, turned on this one event."

"So, you're saying that my father took personal responsibility for the whole war? He blamed himself for the defeat of South Vietnam?" Anh asked.

"In small parts, yes. Your father's nature was to magnify responsibility, like glasses, and accept more than fair amount of guilt."

Anh sat speechless for a long pause as she let this information sink in. "Thank you, *Chú* Lu, for all of your help."

"Would you like me to write this out for you?"

"I would be grateful if you could," Anh said. "I am having a tough time believing what you have just told me about my father."

Lu nodded. He closed the book and studied its binding. He then looked up at Anh and said, "This is a real treasure from your father. You are lucky to have found it."

"I'm not so sure right now, with what you have said."

"Your father, a great man."

Anh dug around in her pocketbook. "I found this, too." She held out a small olive-green patch with two silver blossoms embroidered above a gold bar.

"*Trung tá*, lieutenant colonel. I never knew."

"Mother said he was a captain in the army."

"This must have been his, and he kept to himself. He was promoted."

"Why wouldn't he tell anyone?" Anh asked.

"I don't know. He should have been proud of rank."

"I also found this." Anh presented a tattered red military ribbon, an inch and a half long and one-quarter inch wide. Yellow bars on each end flanked a circular pattern in the center.

"*Bảo quốc Huân chương*," Lu said. He put his fingertips on his temples. "Your father was hero. The badge of National Order of Vietnam—highest military honor award." He reached out to hold the ribbon in his hand.

"What does this mean?"

"Your father must have done thing so great and important for our country that he was recognized with this award. I don't understand why he kept this secret. Perhaps he did not feel worthy of being granted honor."

"I don't understand, *Chú* Lu."

"I don't either. Your father put himself great risk when carried these small strip of cloth and journal out of country. They tell him as officer and hero. Their discovery by North before your escape would have been death for your father and great harm to you and your mother."

"I didn't know."

"Do you think your mother suspect he was awarded National Order?" Lu asked.

"No, *Chú* Lu. I don't think so."

"You need to tell her. She would be proud of Dung."

"Not yet. Can you keep this between us for a little while? I need to think this through."

"Yes, *Cháu*."

Lu handed the ribbon back to Anh as she thought of what her next move should be.

CHAPTER 17

September 24, 1993

The afternoon sun dropped low in the western sky, lighting the underside of fluffy clouds with salmon hues. Rex walked along the top of the seawall, heading home after his first week of work at the Ford dealership. His muscles ached from lifting boxes of engine oil, rolling tires, and pushing a broom around the service bay. It was a feeling—a taste of a hard day's work—he hadn't felt in many months or years. Matt had advanced him a week's pay in cash to buy some shoes and clothes. He was grateful for the generosity of his old friend.

Rex sat on the apex of the concrete wall, which descended like stepped bleachers to the turbid water of the bay, seven feet below. The water was calm except for the intermittent wake of passing boats. Small wavelets marched towards him in orange ranks as the last rays of sunlight bounced off their leading edge, leaving a shadow to follow.

Now that Rex had time to reflect on all that had transpired in the past week, he had difficulty controlling his thoughts. His head was swimming with facts, possibilities, solutions, problems. What-ifs? And whys? His mother used to call this state of mental confusion "monkey-mind."

Rex watched the swells, one right after the other, bend the water's surface and lap against the concrete wall. For a moment, the green-brown water rose from one step level to the next. Gray and white barnacles, exposed by a low tide, coated the nether portion of the seawall. The evening rays on the back of his shirt and neck felt pleasant. Rex closed his eyes to let his senses pull in his surroundings to calm his chaotic mind—the smell of the ocean, the sound of the waves, and the warmth of the sun.

"Rex?" A woman's voice sounded from behind him.

Rex turned and opened his eyes to see Nancy and a small white bouncy dog walking toward him along a dirt path, which followed the shoreline. He hadn't seen Nancy in over a year.

"Oh, hey." Rex struggled against his sore muscles to stand. "Wow, Nancy, what a surprise."

"Yeah. I didn't expect you."

"Well."

"Rex, I've been worried. Nobody seemed to know what happened to you. How long have you been in town?"

"A week or so. Staying at my old place with Jake and Pigeon . . . until I git back on my feet."

"I see." Nancy picked up the little dog in her arms. "Excuse me. This is Rocky."

"Rocky?"

"Yeah. We were just out for a walk. The dog sits at the house all day while I'm at work and can't wait to go romping when I get home."

"Nice to meet you, Rocky," Rex said. He patted the hyper-energetic little dog's furry head and tried to avoid getting licked. Rex didn't care much for dogs, especially little jumpy ones.

"I'm bone-tired at the end of the day and just want to get off my feet. But he keeps me young. Rex, you look good."

"I'm not so sure."

"I'm happy to see you're back home," she said.

"I think I'm happy to be back."

"Sure."

"Things were rough as a cob when I left. You knew that. I got myself straightened out. I've been sober nine months now."

"Yeah. Good for you." Nancy stepped over to the top of the seawall next to Rex. "Do you want to sit? I don't mind talking."

"You don't have to concern yourself with me."

"I said, I don't mind."

"Okay, we can sit a bit."

Nancy took her little dog off the leash and turned him loose to run about the grassy field at the top of the wall. Rocky recognized the spots where he wanted to stick his nose and catch up on any *doggy-news* that had passed since he was last there. Nancy seemed to know her dog would not wander far.

"How're your boys?" Nancy led off.

"Not good. They ain't working. I left 'em in a bad state. I'm not sure what I was thinking. You know I lost the boat?"

"Yeah, I heard."

"Not much for a shrimper to do with no boat."

Nancy stepped down one level on the seawall and sat on the top, looking out over the bay. Rex did the same.

Rex said, "Well when that came to pass, I was in sorry shape. Booze caught up with me, and I was flat broke. Just gathered a few things, caught a ride north, not knowing where I was headed."

Nancy continued to look at the water and said nothing. Rocky came scampering back and licked Rex's hand, which he had propped behind him.

"Run 'long, Rocks," Nancy cried, shooing the little dog away. "Where'd you go?"

"Pennsylvania, Scranton. No reason. I knew a guy in the service once from those parts, and he always talked about how nice it was."

"Was it?" Nancy turned to Rex.

"It was what I needed. I felt guilty about leaving the boys." Rex paused. "I got a job. I cleaned up."

"Good for you."

"I thought my leaving was best for 'em. Now that I'm back, I'm not so sure. Enough of me. What about you? How's the shop?"

"Same, Rex. Same as it's been for the last twenty years. Coffee, eggs, biscuits, grits, nothing changes. People sometimes come and go."

"Like me."

"I have my regulars, but they're slowly dying off. Young folk come in, but I think they're looking for something else, you know, fancy coffee, Egg Beaters. I'm too old for change."

Rex and Nancy sat in silence for several minutes, watching shadows from the last rays of sun climb up the pine trees across Back Bay. On the breeze, a flight of seagulls moved up the shoreline to find a sheltered beach to spend the night. Sunset was the time of the day Rex enjoyed the most. He was happy Nancy had come along to share it with him.

"Pigeon and Jake got themselves in a little bind," Rex started to say but then thought better of it and stopped talking. He needed someone to talk to about his sons and the drowning of Don Nguyen. *Not yet*. Keep your mouth shut, he told himself. Think of the boys. It will not help them now if he spreads rumors.

"How so?"

"Ah, you know, they didn't do so well when I was gone. They didn't have the boat to work. Nothing good filled a lot of idle time. They kind of take after their father, don't ya think?"

"Don't be so hard on yourself. You have always loved those boys, even when you couldn't love yourself. Things will get better. You're better." Nancy pulled her knees to her chest; the hem of her skirt draped her ankles. She wrapped her arms around her legs. "This all will get better with time."

"I just wish I hadn't screwed up their lives so much. You're right. I have always loved 'em, wanted more for 'em. I was doing pretty good when they first come and live with me. What was that, eight years ago?"

"Something like that."

"It's been eleven years we've known each other," Rex said.

He had always enjoyed a closeness to Nancy. Not a physical attraction but a desire to be in her presence. Something about her soft voice, her casual way of listening, and how she handled herself attracted him. Ever since they first met, he felt this about her but knew he was not the man for her. He had too many issues with his life. He couldn't expect her to accept him.

"Nancy, if you don't take unkindly to my asking, why didn't you never git married? I'm sure you had plenty of chances."

"I don't have a good reason. Guess I never found the right one," Nancy said. "I didn't have a great example in my own family. My daddy died a drunk, never kind to my mother."

"Sorry. Your momma still living?"

"No, she passed last year. She was an emotional wreck, battered. I didn't want the same for me."

"I'm a drunk," Rex said, turning to Nancy for a moment before gazing out across the water to the far shore.

"You're an alcoholic and will always be one. Whether you're a drunk is now up to you." Nancy also looked out over the water. "You seem to have done good for yourself lately. I have faith in you."

"Thanks."

"You'll continue to do good," Nancy said. "How'd you get off the bottle?"

"That's a long story."

"I have time."

Nancy turned and caught a glimpse of his profile before he twisted his shoulders to face her momentarily. He cast his gaze across the water again.

"Okay, by the time I got to Scranton, I had the shakes. I would have drunk anything if I could have found it. My last ride dropped me off downtown; I had nowheres to go. You don't want to hear this."

"Yes, I do." Nancy put her hand on his knee.

"I began to sweat and git super anxious. I started to see and hear stuff I knew wasn't real: garbage cans walking around in the alleys and asking me questions I couldn't understand, holes in the sidewalk I could fall into, appearing and disappearing at random, and giant black birds pecking my head.

"The next thing I know, I'm in a hospital room, and it's dark. I could see this other bed next to mine in the room with a body in it. I thought it was dead. Then I thought I might be dead, too."

A pontoon boat passed in front of the seawall. Four young children with bright orange lifejackets jumped from seat to seat as a man, whom Rex judged to be their father, held the wheel. A woman, the mother, sat at the back with a drink in her hand. She had an exhausted look—enough of the kids, the sun, the water.

"The man next to me in the hospital room finally moved and groaned. I asked 'im how long I been there, and he says three days. My arms were all full of holes like they'd stuck me with needles. Pincushion-like."

"How long did you stay?"

"I think 'bout two weeks. One day, a lady who worked there came by my room. She says I had two choices: she'd give me a bus ticket out of town, or I go to a shelter. A home, ya know. That afternoon they took me down to the loading ramp in a wheelchair, put me in a van. Took me to the Lifeguard Mission.

"I stayed there a long time. Nice folk helped me out. They got me a job 'round the corner at a fried chicken place—also, good people. The Lifeguard Mission was a kind of church for guys like me who was on hard times. I'm yapping too much?"

Nancy shook her head.

"They had this preacher who would give little talks around mealtimes. He would talk about Jesus, and God, and angels, and such. A good talker—motivational and everything."

"Did you take to all that preaching?"

"Yeah, it really started to sink in. That pastor handed out Bibles to read." Rex pulled the New Testament out of his pocket.

Nancy took the book and flipped through the pages. "You've written all over it."

"I had a lot of time on my hands," Rex said. "I got saved."

"Oh, what does that mean to you?" Nancy asked.

"I found Jesus. Now I want to live a life that's pleasing to God. You know His laws and all."

"Pretty heavy stuff."

"I'm trying. How about you?"

"Catholic. I'm trying, too," Nancy said. "Why did you come home?"

"You know, at first, I wasn't sure. But now I think I missed my boys. Hope to somehow do good by 'em. You know, set a good example. Now, I'm wondering if it's all too late."

"You're a good man, Rex. It's never too late."

Rex looked at Nancy's straight-held shoulders. At that moment, he wanted to reach his arm up and put it around her. It had been a long time since he had embraced a woman. He couldn't remember ever feeling this way before about someone. *She was kind.* He had spent his adult life using women for what they could give him, never giving back. Having Nancy sit by his side stirred emotions he had never felt. Rex sensed his eyes were becoming moist. He was not ready for this, not yet.

"Been nice talking with you, Nancy." Rex stood abruptly. "I hope to see ya and Rocky again soon."

"Yeah, sure," Nancy said, a little perplexed.

Rex shook Nancy's hand, stepped to the side, then marched down the seawall in the opposite direction from which she had arrived. Rocky scampered after him until Rex shooed him away.

CHAPTER 18

September 25, 1993

The rattling of the truck's engine woke Jake and announced Pigeon's departure. Jake rolled out of bed and looked at his watch—eleven o'clock in the morning. Wearing only boxers, he passed his dad's open bedroom door. The bed covers were neatly pulled up and tucked under the pillow.

Jake walked into the front room and found Amber lying on the couch. He stood in the middle of the room, looking at her for a moment. She was sprawled out lengthwise in a contorted position with her hips and legs turned facing the coffee table, and her shoulders turned to the ceiling. Passed out, most likely, Jake thought. He grabbed a Coke from the icebox and sat at the dinette where he could watch her.

Amber had turned twenty-one the previous month. Her long-awaited birthday didn't change much in her life, except she could now use her real ID—instead of a fake one—to buy tequila, her drink of choice. She never attracted Jake. She was rude, sarcastic, and overweight. Jake thought Amber always showed too much of her pasty skin with her preference for skimpy clothes. This morning she had on a pale-yellow camisole and jean shorts. Jake noticed her hair color had changed again since he had last seen her. Now her chin-length crop was copper-red. He could not remember ever seeing her natural shade.

Jake watched Amber sleep. She had spent the night on the couch before, usually after a fight with her boyfriend. But sometimes she just came over to party with Pigeon. Jake wondered which it was this time. He had no doubt that Pigeon and Amber slept together, now and then. Why Amber's boyfriend tolerated this was a mystery to him. It made no sense. Pigeon could get a girl of his own and not have to share this slut if he wanted. It was none of his business, he thought. But then he's the one who had to deal with her in the house this morning.

It was Amber's boyfriend who got her and Pigeon started on meth. Her boyfriend had been smoking and popping for several years and knew someone in George County who cooked. Jake always thought Amber's boyfriend would move on to heroin if he could get it. But meth was easy to find and gave a fantastic high. Plus, it made you horny—a great party drug. Jake decided that weed would be his drug of choice long ago, and he steered clear of the rest.

Jake rose from the chair and toasted two slices of bread, then smeared them with grape jelly. He opened another Coke, sat at the dinette, and continued to watch Amber take slow, shallow breaths. What a mess he and Pigeon had themselves in. Now that their dad had moved back in with *do-gooding righteousness*, this boil would eventually come to a head. His irrational, hot-headed brother would do something stupid—pick the wound and spill the pus.

Amber stirred, then awoke with a shudder, and scanned the room. She looked at Jake. "Where's Pige?" she asked, rubbing her eyes.

"I was going to ask ya the same damn thing. Pulled out half an hour ago. Don't know where."

"Shit." Amber sat up and ran her fingers through her hair, staring across the room at a blank wall for several seconds. She stood, adjusted the straps on her top, then walked back to use the toilet. "Git me a Coke," she said when she sat back down on the couch.

Jake opened the fridge and pulled another out. He flicked the tab and set it on the coffee table. He sat again at the dinette, facing her.

"Heard your daddy's back, found Jesus and everything," Amber said.

"Came in last week. I'm not sure how long he'll stay."

"Odd timing."

"Say what?"

"Odd timing, I said, numbnuts. This has nothing to do with the boat, does it?" She took a slow drink from the can.

"I don't know what the hell you're talking about."

"Cut the crap, Jake. You know what the hell I'm talking about, the *Miss Anh*, the drowning. Don't give me this *I'm all innocent* shit."

Jake stood and faced the kitchen counter. "What'd Pigeon tell ya?"

"Not much, just that you and he needed to settle a score and that it was a *real shame* that the boat just happened to sink," Amber said. "I'm not stupid. Two plus two equals . . . you sank the boat, dipshit."

"You shut your got-damn mouth." Jake turned to confront her.

"I'll say what I want." Amber stood.

Jake lunged and grabbed Amber's shoulders, holding her at arm's length. "You don't know what the hell you're talking about."

Amber spun, slipped Jake's grip, and slapped him across the face with her right hand. "Keep your goddamn hands off me. Touch me one more time, I'll kill you."

"Fine, bitch."

"I'm out of here. I'm done talking to you." Amber grabbed a soiled canvas purse off the floor and slung the thin strap over her neck and between her breasts. She turned to Jake, "Tell Pige his brother's an asshole, and I walked myself home." Amber let the screen door bang shut on her way out.

It had happened, Jake thought. Pigeon had already bragged. Rumors had started sooner than he expected. He would not take the rap, not if he could help it. With his balled fists, he wanted to hit something. Jake stepped into his bedroom, reached under the mattress, and pulled out the revolver. The cold black grip of the Ruger Security-Six .357 Magnum felt powerful in his hands. He put on a pair of cargo shorts and a button-up plaid short-sleeved shirt. Jake tucked the gun in the small of his back.

Amber was halfway up the curved drive when Jake eventually caught sight of her again. She was five hundred yards from the end of the road and surrounded by dense woods. Though the leaves had started to drop, she remained hidden from the neighbors and the street.

Jake slowed to a quick walk and fell in twenty paces behind her. He pulled the gun out and held it in both hands. He aimed at the center of her back. Amber continued to walk down the tire tracks, unaware she was being followed. Jake flicked the safety and rested his index finger on the trigger. His palms started to sweat. He had never considered killing anyone. The drowning of the Vietnamese guy was an accident. Jake stopped walking. He squeezed the grip of the pistol and felt the pressure build on the tip of his forefinger. He sighted the barrel between Amber's shoulders, right where her thin purse strap crossed the back of her camisole. Pasty white skin, tan strap, sheer faded-yellow shirt, and, he imagined, bright red blood.

Jake froze. He then slowly lowered the gun. He couldn't do it, couldn't pull the trigger. His hands were shaking. He quickly slipped the revolver back into his waistband and straightened his shirttail.

Amber sensed she was being followed, looked behind her, and stopped when she saw Jake. "Stalking me, asswipe?"

Jake replied, "No, I just want to apologize for gittin' in your face."

"Fuck you."

"I think Pigeon went over to Anderson's to do some work today. Said he might."

Amber turned again to walk toward the street then said over her shoulder, "You can let that bastard know I'm no longer his little whore. I'm gone for good."

CHAPTER 19

September 30, 1993 - Noon

Anh stepped into the Jubilee Mission's dining area, scanned the room, and felt immediately out of place. A dozen unkempt men of all ages were sitting on folding metal chairs at white plastic tables and eating in silence. The clicking of forks against tin trays was all she heard. She stood motionless in the doorway, wearing a smart suit with a gray skirt and a white ruffled blouse. The area had an odor of chlorine, roast beef gravy, and urine. She had never been to a soup kitchen, never been in a place like this with homeless men.

The lunch counter on her right was empty except for several large pans of steaming water. A tall black man came out of a door behind the service area. He had a white apron and T-shirt stretched over his muscular chest and shoulders.

"Can I help ya, Miss?" the man asked, pulling a dishrag from his apron string to wipe his hands and forearms.

"Yes, I'm looking for a Mr. Rex Thompson. Someone told me I might find him here today."

"Rex, there's a missus here to see ya," the man shouted through the service door. He turned to Anh and said, "Please sit. Have ya ate? Coffee?"

Anh shook her head politely. "No, thank you."

Rex, also wearing a white apron, emerged from the kitchen and saw Anh. He had never met her but knew who she was and had no doubt why she was there. A brave little girl, he thought.

"Mr. Thompson?"

Rex nodded.

"My name is Anh Truong, and my father was Don Nguyen. I believe you knew him."

"Yes." Rex took off his apron. The mission was not the place for whatever conversation this young lady wished to have with him. "Come with me where we can talk." He opened the door for Anh, then turned and said, "Jefferson, I'll finish up in the kitchen when I git done. Give me a few minutes." He tossed his apron on the counter.

• • •

Nancy's Café was empty; the lunch crowd had disappeared in the late afternoon. Rex and Anh sat in a booth, facing each other.

"I'm sorry to hear about your father. I never really knew him, but I had heard he was a fine gentleman," Rex started.

"My mother and I miss him very much," Anh said.

"Please give my sympathies to your mother for me. Would ya?"

"Mr. Thompson, I'm here to give you this." Anh slid a large manila envelope across the table to Rex.

A young waitress appeared. "Hi, Mr. Rex. Coffee, or can I get y'all something else?" She glanced at Anh.

"Miss Anh, would you like something?" Rex asked. Anh shook her head. Rex turned to the waitress and said, "Angie, I'll take a cup of coffee, black. That's it."

Angie flipped over a mug and filled it from a pot.

"Nancy not working today?" Rex asked.

"Sure, she just stepped out for a bit while it was slow."

"Thank you, sweetie." Rex turned back to Anh and picked up the envelope. It had the fresh chemical smell of a Xerox machine. "What's this?" he asked.

"A journal. Your name's in it."

"You don't say?"

Rex pulled out a sheaf of papers. The first were photocopies of small sheets with Latin script containing many diacritic marks. From his time in the war, Rex recognized the handwriting as Vietnamese. He looked at the remaining pages, typed, double-spaced, and in English. Rex looked up at Anh. "Please. What does this have to do with me?"

"My father, you knew him as Captain Dung in Da Nang—"

"Yes." Rex wondered how much Anh knew about the crime he committed there.

"He wrote this," Anh said, pointing to the gray photocopies, "shortly after he escaped a North Vietnamese prison camp."

Her words stung. He sat motionlessly and listened.

"I knew nothing about this until after he died, and my mother spoke to me. Mother believes you caused my father the great pain that he carried the rest of his life. She is of the forgiving type and wants to forgive you. I think she has already. She said my father told her he had much anger directed toward you for what you did. She believed him. This is not the whole story, Mr. Thompson. I don't think it was anger that troubled my father.

"I recently found a little book, like a journal, among some of his things in a box. I can't read Vietnamese, so I had it translated. Mr. Thompson, my father was a good man and fought bravely for his country. He wrote this in April 1972. I brought these copies for you to read because you were part of his story." Anh spread out the typed pages until she found Rex's name highlighted in yellow. "My mother knows nothing about this journal or the magnitude of the burdens I know my father bore. It would hurt her too much to read it now. If she has already forgiven you, perhaps it is best to leave it at that."

Anh sensed a quiver in her voice. She had rehearsed what she wanted to say when she confronted Rex. But this was much more stressful than she had expected it would be.

"This is all so new to me," she said. "I am not sure what to think. I cannot forgive you, not yet, at least."

Rex glanced down at the papers scattered on the table, then up to the pretty, young woman seated across from him. She had moist, innocent eyes and looked to be fighting back an emotional wellspring within her. Long black hair, pulled back in a tight ponytail, framed her smooth olive-shaped face and exposed green jade studs in her delicate ears. She sat upright in the bench seat with her shoulders drawn back and her chin reaching forward. She was strong, righteous, determined, and brave. He had seen these same characteristics in her father, in a Quonset hut two decades earlier.

"My father wanted to talk to you about what had happened to him in the war. But he couldn't bring himself to do it. He wanted to make things right with you and his Lord. But he didn't before he was killed. I'm not bringing you this journal and asking for your apologies; I don't really care. I'm bringing you this, so you will understand why my father avoided you for all these years. Please, Mr. Thompson, don't feel sorry for my mother or me. Feel sorry for yourself." Anh took a deep breath. She had said her peace.

Rex straightened the papers and stuffed them back into the envelope and took care to fold the brass tabs on the clasp. He had no word to ease this young lady's angst. Nothing he could say right then seemed appropriate. He would take the pouch and read its contents later. He already knew the story, or at least the gist. The fragments of the mystery were coming together in his mind. Rex hoped the journal would explain why he was never accused of the theft, why he never saw Don again in Da Nang, and why Don never spoke to him in the ten years, they both lived and worked in Biloxi. He wondered if Anh thought he was responsible for her father's drowning.

"Thank you, Miss Anh. How do they say, 'You have the courage of a tiger'?"

Anh Truong diverted her eyes from Rex, scooted to the edge of the booth, and stood. She spun in her low-heeled shoes and walked out the door. Her black ponytail popped back and forth across her back, keeping time with her quick steps. Through the large front windows of the café, Rex watched her turn and vanish down the street. A knot formed in his stomach, and he felt ill.

"More coffee, Mr. Rex?" Angie asked, holding a full pot. "Fresh."

Rex looked up at her and shook his head.

"You okay?"

"I'll be fine." Rex placed his hand on his thigh and felt for the New Testament's rectangular outline in his pocket. He reached around and removed his wallet. "Thank you, Angie. Give my regards to Nancy when she gets back. Will ya?" Rex put two dollars on the table and left.

CHAPTER 20

September 30, 1993 - Afternoon

"Turn down here. We're going to The Hole," Jake said to Pigeon, who was driving the Ranger up a road, following the east bank of the Biloxi River.

"Who's driving here?"

"Here. Turn here." Jake grabbed the steering wheel and pulled the truck into a sandy trail that led through hardwood trees.

The Hole was a deep pool in a river bend, twenty feet wide, with a sandbar on one side and a steep bank on the other. This was a secluded section of the stream and a favorite place for the idle young to hang out. On most weekends, during the sweltering summer months, a party was going on at the river. It was here Jake and Pigeon drank their first beer, smoked their first joint, and saw for the first time that bikini tops and shorts don't always stay on after diving into deep water.

Pigeon stopped the truck in the soft sand at the top of the bar and opened the door. The air was brisk. Nobody else was at the river. Jake hopped out of the truck and walked down to the water, taking giant steps in the loose, sugar-white sand. He picked up an empty beer can at the water's edge and tossed it into the river. A slow current carried it around a fallen tree and out of sight. Jake bent down and placed his hand in the clear, tea-colored water and found it much too cold to consider a swim.

A frayed and knotted rope hung from a limb above the deepest part of the pool. Remnants of several earlier swings hung from the same branch, evidence The Hole had seen generations of Biloxi kids cooling off on hot days while coming of age and experimenting with sins of adulthood.

He turned and saw Pigeon sit on a fallen tree trunk at the top of the sandbar and light up a cigarette. Jake climbed up the sand and sat on the log's other end.

"What're we going to do now? You got any brilliant ideas in that thick skull of yours?" Jake asked.

Pigeon pulled a folding knife from his front pocket, opened the three-inch blade, and began to whittle on a dry stick. "Don't know, man."

"Agent Necaise came by the house again yesterday and—"

"You told me already. Okay?" Pigeon shot back.

"Yeah, I told ya, and I'll tell ya again. I think the only reason Necaise came back was that someone's talking. Someone opened their pie hole and started jabbering about how we was the ones who sunk the boat."

"Wasn't me." Pigeon ashed his cigarette between his knees.

"Bullshit. Amber came right out to me."

"Didn't tell her," Pigeon said. He continued to work the end of his stick into a point.

"Bull crap, she said she knew. Word's out."

"Not me."

"Dad thinks we done it. I bet Necaise thinks we done it—otherwise, why's he been snooping around again?"

"They ain't got no proof."

"Don't need no got-damn proof if your little jackass girlfriend's saying we done it."

"She's not my girlfriend."

"Whatever you say, Genius."

Jake smoothed out the sand in front of him with his shoe, uncovering an opened condom wrapper in the sand, then buried it again. He looked across the stream to the rope swing and remembered the times, over the years, he and Pigeon had come here—the girls, the beer, the sunburn, and the tea-colored water. Those seemed to be innocent times, fun times. Things were different now, complicated. Jake always expected he and Pigeon could break from the miserable life with their alcoholic father and do better for themselves. Where did they go wrong? Where did they fuck up?

Other kids who hung out at the river somehow graduated from school and landed decent jobs. Hell, Kyle, the biggest stoner of them all, worked as a welder down at the shipyard at forty thousand a year and drove a goddamn Hummer. But Amber didn't make it, and neither did her boyfriend. Kate did well. She got her degree at University and was now an elementary school teacher. Kate was wild back then. She was the first girl Jake ever saw buck-naked when she shed jeans and a halter top to join some older boys skinny-dipping under the swing. Kate had slender brown arms and legs, a small perky chest, and long straight brown hair. She was married now to a football coach and expecting her second child. Jake smiled when he thought about Kate swimming naked in the river and giggling.

"I'm not doing no time," Pigeon said as he launched his stick like a spear into the pool fifteen feet away. The branch slipped into the water with a thin splash, then popped up to the surface and floated downstream.

"Nobody says ya was."

"Thinking 'bout going to Florida or somewheres."

"That's not smart, you jerk. Necaise will think you're hiding somepin. They'll track ya like a coon dog," Jake said.

"I can't stay 'round here." Pigeon flicked his cigarette butt into the sand in front of him.

"Listen, just play it cool, man. Nobody's pinning this on us. We've got to hang together."

Pigeon picked up another branch from behind him and started to shave the bark off with his knife. The sun dropped below the treetops across the river. Streaks of gold light filtered through breaks in the canopy to highlight the far bank's dark woods. A cool breeze came upstream and stirred the tall grass behind them. They sat in silence.

Jake then said, "Nobody was supposed to drown. I just can't figure why that old man just didn't git off the damn boat with Timmy. How can ya not know how to swim if you're a shrimper?" Jake picked up his own stick and poked about in the sand. "The boat was just supposed to go down, ya know, ruined and shit. The drowning was an accident and technically Don Nguyen's accident. You got to know how to swim if you're a shrimper. Stupid shit. This ain't no murder; it was an accident."

"What ya talking like that for?" Pigeon said. He whacked the log between them with his stick. "I'm not confessing to no accident, and sure as hell not taking the rap for murder."

"We could plead out, ya know . . ."

"I'm not bending on nothing, Jake."

"All right, we keep quiet, and this shit will pass. Remember, they ain't got nothing on us, just like we planned. If you leave, Pigeon, Necaise will find your sorry ass, and it ain't going to look good for nobody."

CHAPTER 21

September 30, 1993 - Evening

It was quiet in the public library except for a hushed conversation at the circulation desk and little laughs from the children's book area. Rex finished reading Don's journal, put the last page down on the table before him, and stared off into the stacks at the far end of the room. A heaviness of guilt, sorrow, remorse, failure, and helplessness cloaked him like a thick robe. Pressure, descending from the top of his head and shoulders, squeezed his arms to his sides. His back felt like it was bending under an invisible load. His legs, weak. The room darkened.

Despair. Death. Torture. Ocean water filled the engine room until the last pocket of air washed out. He closed his eyes.

Against the back of his eyelids, the flashes of tracer rounds were blinding. Under the jungle canopy on a moonless night, the darkness of a four-foot bamboo cage was beyond black. The yellow, red, and blue of hot pokers pressed into the flesh were as if they were searing the sockets of his own eyes.

Open your eyes. Keep them open. Rex studied the shelves across the library again, lit with fluorescent bulbs from a low ceiling and filled with books.

Rex had no idea Don Nguyen had suffered so much because of him.

He could not fathom the feelings of guilt that Don must have carried once he realized his actions sabotaged the armored brigade's retreat at the Se Pone River. For how many deaths of his countrymen did he assume blame? If these were Don's millstones, they were now Rex's as well.

Rex wanted to undo many things. So many failures. Rex wanted to be a good father but failed. Deborah despised him. Jake and Pigeon had no respect for him, but who would blame them? For many years he had no respect for himself or anyone else. Oh, how he wished he could start over. He had cleared his trail from Da Nang to Galveston and Biloxi with a wrecking ball.

Rex closed his eyes again, and the images of the war snapped back.

He raised his lids and looked at the papers stacked next to the manila envelope. His thoughts turned to Anh Truong and her mother, whom he had never met. The anguish and pain he felt now could only be a fraction of what these two women must have lived with every day for the past six weeks. How much stronger were these women than he was?

A young boy about fifteen, wearing a green polo shirt embroidered on the front with a school emblem, stood across from Rex at the other end of the library table. Rex couldn't read the logo, but it looked to be that of a church school. The boy had short blond hair, combed with a part.

"Mister, can I sit here?"

Rex nodded yes, and the boy slung a heavy book bag from his shoulder and sat.

Rex worried again about his own two sons and how he had failed them. He had not been around to raise them into adulthood. Rex was either working on the boat or sitting in a bar.

The boy across the table pulled out a small cassette player, put on headphones, and pressed the play button. Rex could hear music leaking out from the small, padded speakers. The boy opened a heavy calculus book and began to study. His parents must be proud, Rex thought. Perhaps the boy didn't have a deadbeat alcoholic father like himself.

Rex sat in silence, still feeling the weight of the invisible cloak weighing him down. He looked again at the papers in front of him. Time seemed to stop. He wanted to shut his eyes and wake up in another world, but he couldn't face the images on the back of his lids. He stared at the shelves full of books and wondered if they contained the answers to his screwed-up life. Why hadn't he read them? Why had he considered he was always too smart for books and learning and listening? Jake and Pigeon were the same. He had no doubt now his sons were the ones who sank the *Miss Anh*.

He could guess how they did it. How they motored out to the bay in the little skiff he kept down by the water. How they rowed the last bit undetected, and then one of them—Pigeon because he was the stronger swimmer—jumped into the water and looped the cable around the prop. At the same time, Jake attached the other end to the anchor line. They probably even used the old length of wire he kept under the house. Rex thought about his boys taking it upon themselves to sink the boat. Was it revenge? Were they trying to prove something to each other or him? Had their lives sunk to the same depth as his? Was it the Vietnamese? Did they not want anyone else to use what had been theirs? Rex had no answer.

He watched the boy across the table press another button on the tape player, flip the cassette, hit the play button again, and sink back into his book and music. Rex gathered the sheets of the journal and slid them into the envelope. He closed the clasp and laid the packet down. He took the New Testament copy out of his shirt pocket and started to thumb through the pages, not knowing what to look for. He closed his eyes and squeezed the book to his chest. A feeling of warmth and hope came over him. Tonight, he would pray for an answer. He would pray for the young girl, Anh, and her mother. He would pray for Don Nguyen. He would pray for Jake and Pigeon. He would pray for himself, for strength.

"You okay, Mister?" the boy asked as he pulled his headphones off and stared at Rex.

Tears streamed down Rex's cheeks; his head jerked back and forth. Rex opened his eyes and stared at the boy for a long time.

"I'm fine. Thank you, son," Rex said. He put the small book in his shirt pocket and seized the envelope. Rex stood to leave and then said to the boy, "You are the sum of your choices."

The boy fixed a bewildered look on his face as he watched Rex walk out of the room, then dropped his gaze and focused again on the textbook before him.

CHAPTER 22

October 1, 1993 - Morning

It was mid-morning when Matt decided to check on the whereabouts of his friend. Rex had failed to show up for work at the dealership, the first time in the past two weeks. Matt drove a blue Taurus with a yellow dealer plate down the long drive to the camp. Brush scraped against the shiny door panels, like fingernails on a blackboard. Matt was already irritated by having to look for Rex, and the sound of branches marring his new car made it worse. He pulled up to the house and saw the Ranger parked outside. He recalled selling this truck to Rex eight years ago. It was old then, and it surprised him to see it still used now. A faded and peeling sticker on the rear bumper read SAVE YOUR SHRIMP INDUSTRY, GET RID OF THE VIETNAMESE.

Matt was just north of three hundred pounds and had difficulty pulling himself out of his sedan. He climbed the house steps using the rickety handrail, opened the screen, and rapped on the door.

Pigeon cracked the door. "Yeah?" The door shut.

"Pigeon, open up. I'm looking for your dad. You know where he's at?"

The door opened again. Pigeon stepped out on the porch, buttoning up his shorts and pulling the edge of his T-shirt down. "I have no frickin' idea," he said. "Beats me. Why?"

"He didn't show for work."

"What do I look like, his babysitter?"

"I'm worried. Not like 'im," Matt said.

"Told ya, I don't know."

Matt looked at the two-door truck at the side of the house. "I see you still have the Ranger. Runs okay?"

"It gets us around."

"When you're ready, you come by the lot, and I'll make you a good deal on a new vehicle."

"It look like we's got money burning holes in our pockets?"

"Pigeon, I'm just saying."

"Time for you to leave us alone."

"All right, when you see your dad, tell 'im I stopped by, would you?" Matt turned to step off the porch and realized the railing might not hold his weight. "Pigeon, gimme some help."

Pigeon stepped down with his bare feet and offered his arm to Matt. It was then that Pigeon noticed the skiff, kept down at the water's edge, was gone. Jake would have no reason to take it out. The thought that someone stole it came first to his mind.

Matt noticed Pigeon looking toward the water. "What's up?"

"The boat's gone."

"What?"

"The got-damn little boat that Dad keeps for crabbing, it's gone," Pigeon said.

The notion of the cops taking the boat as evidence then entered his mind. But they would need a search warrant, right? You can't just take a man's stuff like that even if you're the police. Pigeon was getting an uncomfortable feeling about the boat. He was sure Matt had his suspicions about the *Miss Anh,* and they probably included him, Jake, and a skiff.

Matt squinted through the trees. "Look, there! What's that?" He pointed.

Pigeon moved to get a better view and saw a small boat in Back Bay about one hundred yards offshore. Both men scrambled down the muddy path to the bank and looked out. The skiff was sitting empty and rocking in a stiff chop. The oarlocks were empty.

Suddenly, the freeboard closest to them rose two feet out of the water for a moment, exposing the boat's flat bottom, then slammed back down with a splash. Again, the hull rose for a few seconds and then fell.

"Someone's trying to git in the damn boat," Pigeon said.

"I don't see nobody. You think they fell out?"

"Shit, of course, they fell out, and they're going to swamp the damn thing if they keep trying to climb from the side."

"Rex?" Matt asked.

"Who the hell knows." Pigeon pulled off his shirt, ran down the narrow pier, and dove into the shallow water.

Matt watched from the shore as Pigeon swam with powerful strokes out to the skiff. A brisk northerly breeze kicked up steep one-foot waves, just short of whitecaps. Pigeon's head and shoulders dropped into the troughs and were momentarily lost to Matt's view as he swam. Eventually, Pigeon grabbed hold of the gunwale and rested.

Matt could think of nothing to help. He hadn't even tried to swim in the past several years. Just the quick walk down to the water from the house had him winded. Sweat was building on his forehead and the back of his neck. He worked his way through the salt grass and sat on the edge of the pier.

Matt looked out to the skiff again and saw no one. They must both be on the far side behind the boat, he thought. Then Matt watched the skiff turn with its bow facing back toward the shore. He could barely make out two heads bobbing in the water at the side of the boat with hands holding on to the rail—the craft listed to one side.

• • •

"You're fucking drunk," Pigeon said, as brackish water splashed off the skiff's freeboard and into his face.

"Thanks, Pigeon, coming out . . . think I could've gotten in . . . by, by myself," Rex slurred.

"You're full of shit. Just hold on."

"I'm holding, been doing this . . . lot longer than you."

"Listen, I'd have no problem leaving your ass out here to drown."

Pigeon looked around to see if any other boat was around to help. It was a chilly mid-week morning, and few recreational boats would be out. No commercial craft came through this section of the bay. At least the wind was coming down the channel and not off the shore, Pigeon thought.

"Dad, move back and hold on. I'm going up front. Just hold on and kick." Pigeon had never talked like this to his dad, never commanded him to do anything in the past. It felt odd.

Pigeon helped Rex slide back to the stern and grab hold. He then swam to the front and pulled a line off the bow. Pigeon tied a loop in the rope and placed it over his head and around one shoulder. He began to swim for shore. In twenty-five yards, he hoped to touch bottom and walk the rest of the way.

The strain on the line from the boat and Rex's dead weight suddenly let up. The skiff slid with the wind to the south. Pigeon looked back to see his father's head, free of the boat, vanish behind a wavelet.

"Grab the damn boat," Pigeon yelled.

He then saw his father's arms go up in the air and sink beneath the surface. Pigeon swam back to where his dad went under and reached down into the dark water. Nothing. Bubbles rose all around him, and he dove. This time he met a crushing grip, and he pulled his father up. Rex gasped for air, then looked at him in such a way Pigeon could not tell whether he was grateful for or disappointed in his rescue.

Pigeon pulled the skiff over while holding his dad's head above water. He took another line from the boat and tied it around Rex's chest and under his arms. He hoisted the rope up and clinched it to both stern cleats, lashing Rex tight to the transom. Pigeon then resumed his pull at the bow until he could touch the bay's muddy bottom with his bare feet.

• • •

Amber ran down from the house when she saw Pigeon pulling the skiff through shallow water toward the shore.

"What's going on?" she asked Matt. Amber wore only flip-flops, gym shorts, and a man's long-sleeve shirt buttoned halfway up the front.

"I don't know. It looks like Rex may have fallen out of the boat. Pigeon's bringing 'im in," Matt answered.

Amber hurried out to the end of the pier and grabbed the skiff when it came close. Pigeon untied Rex and lifted his left arm with his shoulder. He walked him to the shore and laid him down on his back. Pigeon then waded back into the water, reached into the boat, and pulled out an empty fifth of Seagram's Seven. He tossed the bottle on the bank next to his father.

"He's a worthless piece of shit." Pigeon said, looking at Matt. "Thought I wanted 'im back, but I was wrong. He's all yours."

Pigeon then picked up his shirt and took Amber's hand. They walked back to the house, leaving Matt sitting on the pier, and Rex passed out in the grass.

CHAPTER 23

October 1, 1993 - Afternoon

Timmy Truong opened the door. "Agent Necaise, come in. Thank you for coming by. Mrs. Nguyen is expecting you." The young man moved aside.

Necaise stepped into the Nguyen living room, where Linh greeted him with a slight nod.

"Good Afternoon, please sit down, Mr. Necaise." She gestured to him to sit in the upholstered chair.

Shortbread cookies and steaming black coffee were already set out on the table in front of him. Linh glanced at Timmy; he excused himself and went through a door to the back of the house. The widow was no longer dressed in white. She wore a colorful robin-blue *ao ba ba,* a traditional, tight-fitting tunic over baggy black silk trousers. She sat on the front edge of the other upholstered chair, facing Necaise. They were alone.

"Thank you for the coffee—you remembered," Necaise said, lifting the delicate cup.

"Mr. Necaise, it has been hard for me these past few months. I have been thinking about what you said. I know of no one with a reason to sink the boat or kill my husband." Linh shifted in her chair. "I don't know if this is important, but Dung came to the United States from

Vietnam with a secret only he and I knew. I just told Thi Anh. You should know it too."

"Please, go on," Necaise said.

He took out a notebook and pen and listened to Linh tell Don's story in vivid detail. She spoke in hushed tones with a high but pleasant voice, in perfect English, and without pause or stammer. Necaise could tell she was a woman of incredible intellect and grace. Linh stitched together the stories of how her husband had discovered Rex Thompson stealing money from the South Vietnamese Army, the North Vietnamese prison camp, the last few years of the war.

Necaise tried to keep up with his notes, and he dared not stop her and ask any questions. She talked about how Don wanted to forgive Rex for what he had done, tell him face-to-face, but never got the chance. She had found the strength in her faith to forgive Rex twenty years ago. But now, after someone murdered her husband, she didn't know what to think—who to trust and who to forgive.

When she had finished talking, Necaise took a sip of his coffee. It was cold.

"Can I get a fresh cup for you?" Linh asked intuitively.

"No. No, thank you." Necaise looked down at his notes. He had scribbled only the highlights. She would have to come by the office later to go over this again. "Why did you and your husband keep this story secret?"

"Dung was a very private man. There was no need to carry this forward to our new home in America. All was going well until he saw Mr. Thompson again in Biloxi."

"They never spoke to each other?"

"No, never. Dung was angry about what had happened, but he eventually realized he had to forgive Mr. Thompson if he were to move on with his life."

"Do you think Rex Thompson shared this anger?"

"No. I don't think he had any reason to hate Dung for what happened in Vietnam. Mr. Thompson wouldn't know what Dung went through because of him."

"Do you think Mr. Thompson, or his sons, had any problem, in general, with the Vietnamese here?"

"I really don't know how they felt. Dung didn't have any recent problems with anyone. Things have settled down in the past several years," Linh said. "I've never met Mr. Thompson or his sons. I don't know what they think about us."

"So, there's nobody you know who had issues with Mr. Nguyen?"

"No. I hope Rex Thompson is not involved."

Agent Necaise wanted to agree with her. He looked at the coffee table again, studying the intricately carved dragons, pagodas, lanterns, and peasants with conical hats.

"Mrs. Nguyen, how did you and Don get to America?"

"Long story."

"You don't have to talk about it if you don't want to."

"Mr. Necaise, I don't mind telling you if you desire to know."

"Only if you wish."

"I wish."

"I understand that you arrived in Biloxi in the late seventies, but how did you get here from Vietnam? What made you choose Mississippi?"

"At first, I did not want to talk about this with anyone. But time has a way of easing sharp edges in our memories and allowing one to seize a true perspective of one's history, doesn't it?"

"Uh, sure. I agree."

Linh scooted back in her upholstered chair; her small shoes lifted off the floor. She pressed her fingertips together in front of her lips and said nothing for several seconds. Then she opened with, "It was late evening sometime in March 1975, I don't remember the date. Thi Anh and I were staying on the coast near Quang Ngai with the rest of Dung's family: his mother, an uncle, his sister, and a younger brother and his wife and baby. At that time, I did not know where any of my family had gone. Weeks before I had heard that most of my relatives had traveled south to Saigon, I did not know for sure. Around Quang Ngai, the North Vietnamese Army was closing in on us from all directions. We were losing the war. They had already taken Hue City, and Da Nang was about to fall. Our country was collapsing. The North Vietnamese were brutal to those in the South, especially those who fought, especially the officers. Dung and our whole family needed to leave Vietnam."

Necaise listened to what he expected to be an uplifting story of rescue and relocation to America. He was not prepared for what Linh was about to tell.

"A few days prior, Dung had sent word to wait for him at his uncle's house on the coast. We waited even though we could hear the mortar rounds and gunfire of the approaching enemy in the distance. Everyone we knew was talking about trying to flee. Dung's younger brother protested to the rest of the family. He argued that we should leave immediately and not risk our lives waiting on Dung. It was not my place to say anything, so I prayed silently.

"Late that night, Dung appeared in the doorway, dressed in worker's clothes. He was gaunt and dirty. His eyes revealed the terror and tragedy of the war. I ran to him, and we embraced; I hadn't seen him for three years.

"Right then, the family gathered. Dung lifted Thi Anh in his arms, and we made our way down to the beach where the uncle kept a boat. The men heaved the boat into the water, and we all waded out into the surf and climbed in. Mr. Necaise, this was not a big boat, only about twelve feet long. The nine of us sat on small benches or the bottom of the boat. The uncle started the engine, and we headed east, out to sea."

Linh stopped talking. To Necaise, she looked pensive as if she were sorting out demons in her mind.

Linh continued, "We had no food and only a day's worth of water in the boat. The uncle told us that when the dark shoreline in the west fell below the stars at the horizon, there were only two outcomes to our journey: we would be rescued at sea, or we would perish.

"By the time the sky began to lighten, our fuel was gone, and the little boat drifted in the swells. We were all alone; there was no other boat on the water, no ship, either. I would have been happier if the sun had remained at the edge of the sky because there was no cloud, and we had no shelter from its rays. All day, we baked in the heat. All night, again, we drifted. Our fresh water was gone. When the sun rose on the second day, Dung's niece, the infant, stopped crying. Her mother's breasts were dry. Dung tried to cool her off with seawater and shade her from the sun with his shirt. She was listless. Do you want to hear all of this, Agent Necaise?"

"Yes, please go on."

"At midday, a ship heading our way appeared in the north. Our happiness, however, was short-lived; the infant suddenly died in her father's arms. The uncle took a heavy piece of metal from a tool chest and tied it up with the baby in a blanket. He then lowered her over the side of the boat just as the ship approached. Her name was Hai."

Linh stopped talking and looked down at the coffee table. Necaise saw her take a deep breath and swallow hard.

"We were hoping the American Navy would rescue us, but this was not a cruiser. It was a rusted cargo ship, and I saw that the decks were already full of hundreds of other people. I prayed that the ship would stop for eight more souls.

"The ship slowed as it came near our boat but never stopped. It approached so near that its bow almost struck us. The crew lowered a rope net over the side, and the uncle tied our little boat to the ship. One by one, we climbed up the rope ladder. When Dung and Thi Anh were the only ones left, Dung cut the little boat loose from the ship and jumped to the rope net with Thi Anh under his arm. She was only four years old. I watched in horror as Dung and my precious daughter were hauled with the rope net onto the ship as they dangled above the foaming sea. *The sea*, that was the baby's name. Hai means *the sea*.

"The ship was crowded with soldiers, women, children, babies, old men, and old women. Someone gave us water, but there was nothing to eat. The stench of human waste and death filled a small deck area where we found space to sit. I can stop."

"No, I want to hear this." Necaise sensed that Linh had never told this story to anyone. It was raw and uncensored, and he felt strange guilt for being privy to it; he couldn't refuse to listen for the same reason a spectator couldn't take his eyes off a car crash.

"I cried dry tears when I found out that the ship was not taking us to the Philippines or Taiwan. We were headed down the coast of Vietnam to Vung Tau; our long journey to freedom had just begun.

"My husband was not a deserter. His army division simply dissolved when the generals fled the battlefield. Defeat, at the hands of the enemy, was inevitable. The soldiers had no ammunition, no food, and expected none. In Dung's mind, the war was over. He fled south with his men to find their families.

"When the ship anchored in Ganh Rai Bay, the South Vietnamese military police would not let us off. We could see the city was swollen with refugees from all over the country, hundreds of thousands. Dung's mother became ill with dysentery. Many people were dying on the ship, and their bodies were tossed into the bay. Some men, probably soldiers, jumped from the boat and tried to swim ashore. They became bodies, too.

"Eventually, after four days, they let us off the ship, and we found food and shelter in the city. It was chaotic in Vung Tau. We stayed there for about two weeks as rumors escalated of the North Vietnamese Army approaching Saigon. We were all afraid of what the Communists would do to us when they overran the capital and took control of our country. One night, Dung and his uncle gathered us together. We were to leave by boat again within the hour. Dung had secured places on a vessel for our whole family with gold jewelry he had secretly carried in a belt.

"We made our way to the dock and waited. A boat, maybe sixty feet long, appeared in the bay and came close. Other people, who saw the boat approach, started to shove and push. Everyone was desperate to leave Vung Tau and Vietnam. The boat lowered a gangplank to the dock, and many people surged forward to clamber aboard. It was then we became separated from the rest of Dung's family—first, his uncle who was carrying his mother, then his younger brother and his wife, and at last, his sister when she lost her grip on the handrail and fell to the water. We never saw them . . ."

Linh stopped talking. She got up from her chair and slipped through the swinging door to the kitchen. Necaise sat in the empty room, not knowing if he should stay or let himself out.

Several minutes later, Linh reappeared, bowing her way through the kitchen doorway. "I'm sorry," she said. "Please forgive my rudeness."

"It's okay. I feel like it was I who was rude and invaded your private space. I'm sorry."

"Bear with me. The story is almost over. Can I get you some hot coffee now?"

"Yes, please."

Linh returned with a hot pot and refilled Agent Necaise's cup. She placed the coffee pot on the table and sat in her chair. "We never saw the rest of Dung's family again; they never made it onboard. The three of us were crammed in with more than a hundred other people. The boat set off for open water, and within an hour, a Navy ship met us. Sailors lowered large cargo nets over the side and hoisted us up, twenty or so at a time. I was happy and sad.

"Two weeks later, the ship dropped us off in Guam, where the American government processed us. After three months, Dung, Thi Anh, and I boarded an airplane for America. I had never flown in a plane before and was terrified.

"They sent us to a camp at Eglin Air Force Base in Florida while we waited for an American sponsor. The Catholic Church in New Orleans supported several families from Eglin. They helped us find a place to live on the city's east side. Dung spoke English very well and soon became the spokesman for our little community.

"Some of the other Vietnamese who lived in New Orleans had been fishermen in Vietnam, and they tried to build or buy little fishing boats to earn money. This did not go well with the locals who already fished those waters. Tensions built, tempers exploded, and we were threatened with violence. Not all Americans welcomed us. Some assumed we were Communists and didn't understand why we had left our country. Dung was caught up in the middle as he tried to translate for everyone."

"How did you get to Biloxi?" Necaise asked. He was swept up in Linh's story.

"In about 1977, the oyster-packing houses needed workers. At first, just a few families moved here to work, but soon dozens followed. Our family moved here late that year. Dung started out shucking oysters but, in a brief time, moved to shrimp. But that is a story for another day. I have taken too much of your time already, Agent Necaise, with my long-windedness."

"No, you haven't."

"I was sad to leave our home in Vietnam, the home that once was. But

I'm happy to be in America with a peaceful future that still might be," Linh said.

"Did Mr. Nguyen share your feelings about America?"

"Yes, he did."

"When Mr. Nguyen started to shrimp, did he have a boat?"

"A little wooden boat he made from scraps of plywood and lumber. I helped him tie our first nets. It's not too hard with a little practice once you get the hang of it."

"You helped with the shrimp?" Necaise asked.

"Sure, we all did. I picked and sorted until my fingertips bled. Dung was a hard worker, and in a couple of years, he bought his first big boat, the *Tien Hai*. It burned."

"So, I have heard."

"That didn't stop Dung. You know he never fought back; he just kept moving forward. People respected him for this." Linh paused and gazed through the sheer white curtains covering a large window in the room. "Dung was a good man. He was good to many people. That is our story."

"Thank you." Necaise was not sure what next to say. He failed to understand much about the Vietnamese who had lived, worked, and worshiped in this coastal town for the past fifteen years.

Getting back to the business at hand, Necaise said, "I don't know where this connection to Rex Thompson will lead, but I appreciate you offering this information. Please realize we are working hard to find your husband's killer, whoever it is. Perhaps something you said today will open some leads."

Linh sat in the chair with her knees and hands together and looked at Necaise. She then nodded ever so slightly, looked briefly to the floor, and said, "Mr. Necaise, I'm sorry to burden you with our troubles. Thank you for listening to me. I know you are a good detective. You will find out who did this." She turned toward the door leading to the back of the house and raised her voice. "Timmy will show you out."

• • •

Necaise did not want to go back to the office right away. He needed time to think, to digest what Mrs. Nguyen had just told him, and to put some of these new puzzle pieces together. He could not shake the images in his mind of Don, Linh, and Anh, escaping to the sea with only a tenuous grip on their hope for freedom.

He stopped his car next to the Oak Street Pier and got out. The dock rose several feet over the water. It extended fifty yards out in the channel, which separated Point Cadet from the nearby portion of Deer Island. Nobody was out on the fishing pier. Necaise walked to the end and found shade under a pavilion where he could watch the boat traffic in front of him. To the left, he could see new construction for the mooring of casino boats and hotels on property once occupied by seafood packing plants. The air out on the water smelled better with the plants gone, he thought. To the right, he could see a man-made, white sandy beach extending to the Biloxi Small Craft Harbor. The county trucked in sand from elsewhere to promote the Coast's image of a beach resort. One had to wade only a few feet into the Gulf water to find a muddy bottom, which oozed up between the toes. Necaise avoided the beach.

Pigeon and Jake were still his prime suspects. Jake seemed nervous last week when he stopped by the house again to talk. He had hoped to catch Pigeon and Rex at home as well but missed them.

The day before he revisited Jake, Sidney told him that the Biloxi Police picked up a kid named Earl Beaugez, Jr., for possession of crystal methamphetamine. His friends called him "Squirrel." He was a small-time peddler. Beaugez was warbling down at the station about how he knew who sank the *Miss Anh*. But he would not say who until the district attorney gave him a deal. It didn't take Sidney more than a few hours to connect Beaugez to Amber to Pigeon, and the DA offered nothing.

But then there was Mrs. Nguyen's story about a crime committed twenty-three years ago by Rex Thompson. This raised a possible motive. Would Rex want to silence Don for what he knew about the money? But Rex wasn't even in the area at the time of the sinking, or was he? It didn't make sense that Rex would want to sink the boat. Why now? He had years to get back at Don if he felt he needed to but never acted.

The boys seemed much more likely to have pulled this off. A cable had to be attached below the waterline from prop to anchor, a two-man job, Necaise reasoned. Plus, Pigeon hung with Amber and Beaugez, and Beaugez wanted to talk. Time to pick up the boys and have a chat down at the station.

Necaise leaned on the rail and looked across the water. A small blue and white boat caught his attention as it made its way up the channel with a squabble of seagulls diving and reeling about its stern. He recognized this as a tourist boat that took passengers out for a shrimping tour on Biloxi Bay. Someone had built the craft to look like a scaled-down commercial trawler. Necaise had never been on a real working shrimp boat before—or a fake one—despite living on the Coast for fifteen years. Maybe, when his nephew comes again to visit from Clarksdale, he would get tickets on the shrimping tour. His nephew would like that.

The blue and white boat slowed in front of the pier, and Necaise watched it haul in a small net. The two-man crew dumped a bucketful of shrimp and tiny fish on a skirted table at the back of the boat. Six or seven adults and an equal number of small children gathered around the table to admire the catch. An old man with a long gray beard and a yellow nor'easter hat—a hat Necaise thought looked ridiculously out of place on the Gulf Coast—stood at the table to sort through the shrimp and fish. He held each new species for the guests to see and said something Necaise couldn't hear. The man with the nor'easter then threw the shrimp into one bucket and the small fish into another. He then took the bucket of silver-sided fish and emptied it in the water, where the gulls descended in frenzied chaos upon this unwanted portion of the catch.

Bycatch, this was what they called it, he remembered—the undesired fish and other sea life caught up incidentally in a dragnet while seeking something else like shrimp.

Necaise turned to walk back to his car. He would cast his own nets tomorrow.

CHAPTER 24

October 2, 1993 - Morning

Agent Necaise followed three Biloxi police cruisers as they turned down the two-track drive. No light. No siren. A ground fog had settled in and around the low-lying areas during the night. The rising sun would soon burn off the mist. On the police radio, chatter among the three cars ahead of him confirmed the takedown at the Thompson place was still on. Lieutenant Reilly, the team leader, rode in the third vehicle and gave last-minute instructions.

Necaise's presence wasn't necessary while the officers arrested Jake and Pigeon. He just thought he would tag along and watch. It had been a long time since he had worked in enforcement and taken part in a raid. He missed the adrenalin rush when the order was given for the team to plunge into danger in the name of public safety. Today he would hang back, watch the action, and maybe get a statement or confession after the arrest.

The cruisers fanned out in the clearing in front of the camp. Necaise stopped his navy-blue sedan at the end of the drive, where he had a view of the front door. Two officers got out of their car and circled to the back of the house with their service weapons drawn, pointing skyward. Two more officers positioned themselves next to the bottom of the front steps, their backs up against the house, ready to climb and breach the door. Lieutenant Reilly crouched behind the open passenger door of his car and checked his pistol. His partner squatted behind the driver's side door and did the same.

Necaise watched all of this unfold through his windshield. Thick fog, however, made it difficult to see the back of the house from his location. He had complete confidence in Lieutenant Reilly, whom he had known for the past five years. Reilly was wise to come in with six officers, Necaise thought. After all, he was going to arrest the boys for murder, and they knew Jake to be armed. Neither boy had a history of violence, but still, you never know how a cornered *animal* will act. He felt the excitement build as the officers, in position, waited for the final order to come in through their earpieces.

• • •

"Jake, wake up," Pigeon whispered through the bedroom doorway. "The whole got-damn yard's crawling with cops. Got guns out." Pigeon stooped low and crab-walked back to the front room to peek out a window again.

Jake sprung from his bed and quickly processed what Pigeon had said. He had decided before if the police ever came to arrest him, he would surrender. The police couldn't prove a thing with their airtight story, he told himself. He had expected Necaise to show up at the house and take him and his brother downtown for a little good-cop, bad-cop questioning and then let them go. He didn't expect what Pigeon had just told him.

Jake reached under his mattress and pulled out the Ruger. He checked to see the cylinder had six cartridges and grabbed a box of spare ammunition from his closet. Jake went prone to the floor and eased himself over to the bedroom window. Through a crack in the blinds, he could see two officers in a position behind trees at the edge of the woods.

Pigeon crawled back to the bedroom, dragging a baseball bat. Beads of sweat were flowing down his face, and his hands were shaking.

"What the fuck's that?" Pigeon asked when he spotted the revolver. "You crazy? You're going to git us killed."

"You see those cops out there?"

Pigeon looked at his brother with disbelief.

"They ain't waiting for us to walk on out like little pansies with our hands up and our pants down. They're coming in with a firestorm and couldn't care less whether your sorry ass gits shot up full of holes."

"They's not doing that."

"The only way we git out of here alive is with this." Jake pulled the hammer back and shoved the gun in Pigeon's face.

"Jake, I don't know. I thought ya had a plan."

"I do, dammit."

"Said we'd git picked up for questioning, that's all. This ain't right. There are four cop cars out front. You're not shooting your way out of this. You lost your fucking mind?"

"I wouldn't be having to do this at all if you'd kept your trap shut."

"Don't blame me," Pigeon said.

"Fuck it. Help me with this." Jake pulled the twin mattress off the bed. Pigeon leaned it across the open bedroom doorway. Jake took the box spring and propped it up on the wall in front of the window behind them. Both men ducked low behind the mattress, where they could watch the front door.

"When they come through, they're going to git a piece of this," Jake said, as he rested the .357 Magnum on the top edge of their flimsy cover. "Here, pull six out and hold 'em." Jake handed the box of ammo to Pigeon.

• • •

Lieutenant Reilly got up from behind his cruiser and dashed back to the blue sedan. Necaise lowered his side window.

"What's up, Lieutenant?"

Reilly put his hand on the roof and leaned into the open window. "You will never believe this shit," Reilly said as he kept his eyes on his officers at the front of the house. "Rex Thompson is down at the station right now, confessing to the *Miss Anh*."

"You're kidding?"

"Nope, I just got word on the radio that he went into the Howard Avenue station and confessed. He just walked in off the street and said he had something to say."

"I'll be damned." Necaise placed both hands on the steering wheel and looked out through the fog to see the two officers at the front of the house, waiting for the *go order*. "What are you going to do now?"

"Arrest him."

"No, what are you going to do about these boys?"

"Call it off. I can't go hauling their asses in when I've got their father confessing to the same crime. The DA would have my own ass. I'm calling it off before these boys get the jitters and do something stupid." Reilly ducked back to his car and grabbed the mic off the passenger seat and began to speak. The four officers around the house pulled back and got into their cruisers.

Better get on down to the station to talk to Rex, Necaise thought.

• • •

"I don't believe you did it," Necaise said to Rex, who was sitting on the other side of a small metal table in the interrogation room.

"I told ya, I did. I sank the *Miss Anh*. I didn't mean for nobody to get hurt," Rex said with a blank expression.

Necaise had interviewed hundreds of killers, rapists, molesters, thieves, and crooks in the past. He could tell when the truth was proffered and when a lie was played. Rex Thompson was lying, and he wasn't even good at it. The man before him was confessing to a crime he could not have committed. Necaise found himself in a unique position, trying to talk someone *out* of a confession. His mind was racing.

"Okay, Mr. Thompson, let's start again when you say you got on the bus last summer. When was that?"

"I left August 12th."

"Now you took the bus from Scranton to Chattanooga, then changed for Memphis and Biloxi, right?"

"Yeah."

"Do you have any proof—like a bus ticket?" Necaise realized the absurdity of the question after he asked it. Of course, someone coming to commit a crime will not keep evidence to prove he came. "You don't have to answer that."

"I got here on August 14th and slept in the woods on the backside of the Point, just down from my house," Rex tried to explain again.

"I got that. Then you saw the *Miss Anh* pull out and take anchor off Deer Island. When was that?"

"The day after I got here. What August 15th?"

"Right. Anyone see you hanging out in the woods?" Again, Necaise thought how stupid the question was. He felt like he was handwriting in a mirror. His whole perspective on this interrogation was *backassward*.

"No one saw me."

Of course, no one saw him. It was a made-up story on how he committed a crime he could not have done. Why would he fabricate breadcrumbs to leave behind?

"Getting back to the *Miss Anh*, tell me again how you got the cable on the prop by yourself." Necaise had seen the wreckage and had a good idea how difficult it would be for Rex to dive with a heavy wire loop and attach it to the propeller blade, at night, in the dark, without making a noise, by himself, at his age—the mental list went on and on.

Rex explained, "I motored in the skiff to the shrimper with that little seven-horsepower kicker I keep under the house. First, I took one end of the cable and attached it to the anchor line with a threaded shackle . . ."

The specific detail that a coupler was used to attach the cable to the anchor line was identified by the divers before they raised the trawler. The presence of a threaded steel shackle had deliberately been kept from the press and everyone else who didn't need to know.

Necaise said, "Let me get this clear. You attached a shackle directly to the anchor rope? You used the shackle as a coupling to connect the cable loop to the two-inch rope, right?"

"Yeah, that's right. I just put the shackle through the loop and then around the rope and screwed in the pin."

How the cable was attached to the anchor line could only be known by the killers, or the killer—Necaise questioned his instincts. He couldn't remember precisely how the divers had found the cable attached to the rope, and he jotted a note to himself to find out. "Go on," he said.

"After I attached one end to the rope, I ran the skiff 'longside the shrimper, letting the cable out. I tied up to a tire bumper at the transom. I took a length of rope I'd brought with me and attached it to the skiff, then passed the rope through the other loop at the end of the cable, two times and . . ."

Necaise was following what Rex said and was almost believing the description of the events was accurate. Absurd, he thought, simply crazy. But the story was sounding genuine to him.

"I climbed out of the skiff and hung on to the bumper with one hand and the rope wrapped around the cable loop with the other. It was dark and quiet in the shadow of the rigging light."

How did he know the light was on that night? Was it just a good guess, or did all shrimpers leave a lamp burning at night? He would have to check on this.

"I let go of the bumper and held on to the rope. The weight of the cable pulled me down under the hull. I was able to control my drop with the rope wrapped around the cable. I let a little rope out at a time. When I got to the rudder, I looped the cable onto one of the blades, and I was done."

"What about the rope?" Necaise knew they found no rope wrapped around the wire. A transparent hole into Rex's story.

"I pulled it off and took it with me. It wasn't tied on to the cable, ya know."

Necaise thought he must sound like a fool. He still didn't believe Rex's story and continued to think Jake and Pigeon had committed the crime. How did Rex know about the cable and the threaded steel hasp? He put together a convincing tale, even to the details of lowering the cable loop onto the prop blade. If his sons committed the crime, then father and sons thought the same. Rex had owned the boat for almost twenty years. Clearly, he knew how to get around it, what to hold on to, and how to find the prop. Hell, he'd probably dove to the propeller many times over the years to cut off an errant line or fouled net.

Necaise leaned forward and put both hands on the table and looked at Rex. "Why're you doing this? Why are you confessing to a crime you had nothing to do with?"

"I told ya I did it. When I got back to Scranton, I saw it on national news. I figured that someone would think that Jake and Pigeon sank the boat 'cuz I used to own it. I couldn't stay in Pennsylvania thinking they's taking the rap. They didn't do it. They's innocent. I came back home, to tell the truth—justice and all, ya know."

"None of this makes a lick of sense. I don't believe one word of your story," Necaise said. "You want to know what I think? I think you are guilty. Not guilty of sinking the *Miss Anh*. No, guilty of screwing up your life and screwing up your sons' lives. But you found God, didn't you? You got saved. And when you came back to make amends with your screwed-up boys, you found out they sank the boat. Not only sank your boat but killed a man who knew your secret from Vietnam. This story never made national news. You learned this when you got back.

"Don's wife told me all about your history with her husband in Da Nang. When you found out the boat sank, did this make you feel all guilty? Guilty of raising Jake and Pigeon to murder Anh's father, the man who looked the other way when you were caught thieving? Did you know that when you got back from Nam, while you were boozing it up and banging your new wife in Galveston, Don was sitting in a bamboo cage in the jungle? Because of you. Did you know that?"

Rex shook his head. He didn't want to admit that he had met with Anh two days ago at the café. Rex suspected Agent Necaise didn't know this yet and was also unaware of the journal.

"You felt guilty. You wouldn't have given a rat's ass if you had found this out while you were still bending and thinking only of yourself. But now that you're with God, everything's changed." Necaise was letting loose, and he was a little embarrassed with his language and tone of voice. Usually, he could hold back, act professional—the good cop. "I told you I don't believe your . . ."

Rex closed his eyes, and heat built in his face. Images from the journal flashed before him. Canes splitting skin in deep red slashes with each blow.

Bamboo cages. His back ached and burned. Shocking pain in his testicles surged into his pelvis from alligator clips attached to a car battery, again and again. The smell of feces, urine, pus, and clotted blood filled his nostrils. His tongue felt thick and dry. Screaming! Someone was screaming in his ears. He could no longer hear Necaise talking. The roar of a fighter jet passed over his head, and he could feel the blow of hot exhaust on his face. A mortar round landed nearby and jolted him to the side of his chair. The *thump, thump* of a helicopter rotor blade paced out the seconds—*thump, thump, thump.*

Rex opened his eyes, focusing on a wall clock across the room. *Tick, tick, tick.* He glanced at Necaise, who was looking at him but said nothing.

Rex wiped his forehead with his shirtsleeve, studying the chrome cuffs on his wrists. He felt trapped. Trapped between Don Nguyen's past, coming at him in tsunami waves, and his newfound faith that was crumbling around him. "You got some water?"

Necaise got up from his chair and poked his head out the door. He sat down with two plastic water bottles and gave both to Rex.

"Listen, Agent Necaise," Rex said after taking a long drink. "I done it. I sank the *Miss Anh*. I feel bad about Mr. Nguyen. I wish it never happened."

"Let's just say for the moment that I believe you, which I don't," Necaise said. "Why do you say you did it? Why did you sink the boat? You knew nobody was going to go after you for stealing money twenty-three years ago. Nguyen wasn't a threat to you. What motive can I use for your sinking the boat?" Necaise placed his pen to paper, ready to write, and looked at Rex. "Tell me."

Rex gazed at the ceiling, his lips moving without a sound as if he were rehearsing a performance. He looked Necaise in the eye. "I had that boat, long time," Rex said. "She's my baby. You're right, and I fucked up my life and the lives of my boys. I always wanted to make things right for 'em, give 'em a good home, teach 'em how to be men, and make 'em better than me. I failed. When I first lost the boat to the bank, I figured I could get it back. You know, get straightened up, make some money, and pay what I owed. When I found out the bank sold it to Mr. Nguyen, I couldn't stand the thought of Jake and Pigeon having to watch our boat come and go all season long, knowing it was never going to be theirs when I was gone. If I couldn't have it, I didn't want nobody to."

IF I COULDN'T HAVE IT, I DIDN'T WANT NOBODY TO, Necaise wrote in bold letters at the bottom of the notepad, and then he underlined the statement.

Necaise looked at his watch. The Biloxi chief of police and the mayor had scheduled a press conference in ten minutes on the steps of City Hall. They were to announce the arrest of the man who allegedly sank the *Miss Anh* and caused Don Nguyen's death. They planned to stand before the cameras just before five o'clock to get local news coverage. Necaise was glad they did not ask him to attend. The police had the wrong man in custody. It would be best if he stayed out of the public's eye.

"I'm done with you today," Necaise said, looking at his watch. "I want to catch the evening news."

CHAPTER 25

October 2, 1993 - Evening

"Thi Anh, can you come and help me with the dishes?" Linh asked her daughter from the kitchen doorway.

Linh, Anh, and Timmy had just eaten dinner without a word spoken amongst them. Anh rose from the dining room table, grabbed the last of the dirty dishes, and left Timmy sipping from a beer bottle. Linh busied herself in the kitchen, putting away jars of spice and leftover food. She then began straightening out cans of pickled baby carrots, straw mushrooms, and beef broth on her pantry shelves. Anh stepped to the sink, filled it with soap and warm water, scraped the remaining food off the plates, and stacked them next to the sink.

"Thi Anh, would you help me with this soy?" Linh asked while kneeling in front of a tub of beans on the pantry floor. "I want to split it up into little bags and give it to the neighbors."

Anh turned from the sink with suds covering her forearms. "Mother, what are you doing?"

"I want to give out some beans."

"No, you asked me to come in and help with the dishes. Now you're off on something different."

"The beans—"

"The beans will be here tomorrow. The dirty dishes will be here, too, if we don't put them up. Come." Anh held out a dish towel for her mother and pointed to the draining board full of clean plates.

Linh stepped next to Anh, picked up a plate from the rack, and began to dry. "I don't know what to think anymore," she said.

"Please, Mom, dry, don't think."

"Your father never thought that man was evil. Your father thought he had made a stupid mistake, one that sent ripples out in all directions, like a stone falling in a pool." Linh stacked the dry plates in a cabinet above her head. "I'm surprised he did it, and I can't control my rage. I'm angry."

Anh knew who her mother was talking about. Both had watched the news earlier in the evening and heard the police chief and the mayor speak.

"You don't know he did it, not yet," Anh said. She rinsed off the drinking glasses and placed them in front of her mother.

"Why would they arrest him if he didn't do it?"

"I don't know."

Anh finished up with the pots and scraped out the wok on the stove. She wiped her hands on the towel her mother used to dry the dishes and then sat at a small round table in the kitchen corner. Anh had sat at this table many times before. For as long as she could remember, she had sat here as her mother fixed breakfast or made spring rolls or fried egg noodles. She and her mother had eaten many meals at this table together when her father was working the boats. But she could not recall her father ever sitting, eating, or drinking in the kitchen. Timmy also rarely came to the kitchen, even after he and Anh married and moved in with Linh.

"Timmy?" Linh asked as she gestured to the dining room and sat next to Anh.

"He'll be okay. He'll go read."

The kettle on the stove began to whistle. Linh got up, filled a teapot with boiling water, and placed it on the table with two white porcelain cups decorated with orange poppy petals and green ginkgo leaves. Anh loved these two teacups her mother brought out only when she shared tea with her. The cups, her mother once told, were from the same town in Vietnam in which Anh's grandmother was born and resembled the cups her mother remembered as a child.

Linh poured hot tea into the teacups and gave Anh the one never broken. The cup Linh always saved for herself showed yellow epoxy in cracks at the handle's top and bottom. Anh had dropped this cup when she was a young girl, and her father repaired it. The rough glue on the inside of the smooth porcelain handle, Linh would say, always reminded her of past times.

"I don't think Mr. Thompson killed Father," Anh said, looking at her mother's teacup.

"I'm sure he didn't intend to."

"No, I don't think he had anything to do with the sinking of the boat," Anh said. She glanced at her mother's face. She has worried, Anh thought. She has worried about her family her whole adult life. Does she still worry about Timmy and me?

Anh then said, "I met with Mr. Thompson last week at a café."

"What?"

"I met with Mr. Thompson."

"Where did you see him?"

"Nancy's. I told him what you had said to me on the bench under the oak tree, what you said about him and father." Anh dared not mention the journal to her mother at this time. She had not fully processed the ramifications of her father's involvement in Lam Son's failure in her mind.

"Thi Anh, I can't believe you would do such a thing. Why?"

"I needed to talk to him. Father never could, and now he never will. I felt I needed to."

"What did he say?" Linh asked.

"Not much. I did all the talking. He said he was sorry about Father, and I believed him."

"Did you tell him your father suffered because of him?"

"Yes."

"Did you tell him your father wanted to forgive him for what he had done?"

"Yes, Mother."

"You don't think he sank the boat?"

"No, Mother."

Lifting the delicate handle, Linh blew steam off the top before sipping the hot tea. Neither mother nor daughter spoke for several minutes.

Anh then said, "My gut tells me he didn't sink the boat and had no idea Father had endured such pain because of him. Mr. Thompson was surprised by what I told him. He didn't know what to say. He just sat there and listened."

"How can you be so sure?"

"I am."

"But you don't know who then?" Linh asked.

"No, but I know it's not Mr. Thompson."

• • •

A correctional officer opened the glass and steel door to the visitation area with a large brass key. Rex shuffled into the room, wearing an orange jumpsuit with HARRISON COUNTY stenciled on the back in large black letters. The guard pulled out another set of keys and unlocked the cuffs on his wrists.

"Sit," the officer said in a voice devoid of emotion and judgment. He pointed to a blue plastic chair in front of a low counter and a small wire-reinforced window.

Rex looked up and saw Jake dressed in street clothes and facing him on the other side of the glass. Rex lifted the handset off the cradle, placed it to his ear, and said, "Nice to see ya, Jake."

"Listen, Dad, you don't need to do this," Jake said into his receiver.

"How's Pigeon?"

"You're screwing things up. Pigeon's gone. Two weeks ago. Left the day you ratted out."

"Why would he leave?"

"Because there was a whole shitload of pork in the yard that morning."

"Cops?"

"They was coming to haul our asses off. Didn't ya know?"

"No. I hadn't heard."

"Pige got scared and left. Don't know why the cops didn't bust the door. Maybe 'cuz you was singing down at the station, fingering your ass about the boat."

"Where'd he go?" Rex asked. He looked at Jake.

"Don't know, and if I did, I wouldn't tell here." Jake glanced around the room.

Several other visitors were talking in hushed voices, with inmates sitting on the other side of the glass partition. On the visitor's side, a single guard stood in the corner of the room and scanned the crowd.

"I think Amber done run with 'im," Jake said. "I laid it open to 'im it would look bad if he split. And, when you got 'round to flipping, or the cops figured you're full of shit, they'd go eyeballing 'im . . . and me."

"You two have nothing to worry about," Rex said.

"Crap, you didn't have to do this for us. Even if the cops hooked us, they'd nothing. Nothing. We'd be walking, two hours tops," Jake said. "Now, you've fucked this all up."

"I hope you and Pigeon can forgive me someday for being such a shitty father."

"That what this's all about? You're feeling all gooey warm inside about how ya reared us? You want to kiss up by taking the rap? That it?" Jake raised his voice then looked at the guard.

"Don't worry about me. This is best."

"I'm not fucking worried 'bout you," Jake whispered. "I couldn't give a shit. I don't care if ya rot in this cage, rest of your born days." Jake again found himself raising his voice, then he whispered into the handset, "Dad, listen to me. I only worry about Pigeon and me. Cut the crap, we all know who done this, said so yourself after talking with Matt. The cops are not stupid. Got-damn it. Eventually, they'll figure you're covering and pinch Pige and me for murder. Hell, they'll probably slap ya an accessory."

"I met with my lawyer, public defender. He's a nice guy. He speaks well and says he can get me off on manslaughter. Good behavior and all, I'm looking at ten to fifteen," Rex said.

A buzzer sounded, and the officer in the corner stepped forward, saying, "All right, ladies and gentlemen, time's up."

Rex placed his palm up against the glass in front of Jake.

Jake spoke into the receiver, "Pigeon, and I was doing just fine when you was gone. Now you've come back and fucked it all up. I want ya to stick to your got-damn fairytale. Hell, I'll even shine your little story and help strap your sorry ass down to your *stainless-steel ride* and help spike your arm."

"If you talk to Pigeon, tell him I'm sorry," Rex said, then he stood and lined up with the other prisoners where he was shackled and led through the same door he had entered. Once all the orange suits had left the area, Jake walked free.

CHAPTER 26

October 18, 1993

A gust of fresh air blew the glass door open as Fred Necaise stepped out of his favorite lunch spot on Howard Avenue. The Fisherman's Catch was a local hangout for bankers, lawyers, businessmen, and anyone else who had offices in downtown Biloxi. Most folk just called it the Catch. The eatery was open only for lunch from eleven to three. Necaise had a weakness for their oyster po'boy, dressed with tomato, shredded lettuce, mayonnaise, and a splash of Tabasco. Oysters from the Gulf were best in the cool months like October, months with the letter *r* in them. He realized he should have eaten a salad or, at most, the baked flounder, something with fewer calories—no sense in telling his wife, or his doctor, what he ate today unless pressed. He would eat a light supper. Necaise strode down the brick sidewalk, back toward his office.

"Agent Necaise."

He turned to see Anh Truong jogging to catch him against a stiff wind in her face. He stopped and extended his hand as she approached.

"Do you have a minute?" Anh gasped, out of breath.

"Sure, Mrs. Truong."

"Please . . . call me Anh."

"Anh, then. Let's get out of the wind," he said.

Necaise led Anh up to the second floor of an art deco building overlooking the Vieux Marché. What was once the bustling center of Biloxi business was now an empty pedestrian-friendly street between historic buildings occupied by struggling storefront ventures and a rotating array of nightclubs—a two-decade failed attempt at urban renewal.

"Thank you, Agent Necaise, for allowing me this time," Anh said, as she sat in a thinly upholstered metal chair next to his desk.

"I'm glad you caught me. How is your mother doing?"

"I guess, okay. She was pretty upset when the police arrested Mr. Thompson; it made my father's murder so real. Do you know what I mean?"

"Of course," Necaise said. "Can I get you something to drink? Tea? Coke? I think there is fresh coffee in the back."

"Nothing. No, thank you."

"Okay, Miss Anh, go on. Why are you here?"

"Mother told you about my father's history with Mr. Thompson. I didn't know any of this before he died. They kept it to themselves. She told you my father wanted to talk to Mr. Thompson but never could. I think, in her heart, Mother had forgiven him years ago. But, now that they have arrested him, my mother is conflicted. She is angry with him and herself for being, in her mind, such a fool."

"I understand. Just because we arrest someone doesn't mean they're guilty," Necaise said.

"I know that. I don't think Mr. Thompson sank the boat."

"Why do you say this?"

"I met with him a little over three weeks ago, right before he was arrested."

"You met?"

"Yes, at a café. I looked for him."

"How did you find him?"

"Down at the Mission. Timmy helped me track him down."

"Why did you want to talk to him then?"

"After my mother told me the same story she told you, I found this."

Anh held out a small tan book. "This is a journal that my father kept after he escaped from the North Vietnamese. He wrote his story here."

Agent Necaise glanced at the book in her hands.

"My mother knows nothing of this journal. I found it in the house after Father died. The details of his imprisonment and torture are graphic. I don't think my father ever intended for anyone to read it, at least while he was living."

"You showed it to Mr. Thompson?"

"Yes, he was mentioned in the journal; I had it translated. I felt that I needed to share it with Mr. Thompson; he was part of the story. There are details about the war written in the journal that my mother does not know and so could not have told you."

Necaise sat up in his chair. "Go on."

"Before the North Vietnamese captured my father, someone deliberately withheld vital information from his group of tanks and such. This put his whole unit in danger unnecessarily. It caused the death of hundreds of South Vietnamese soldiers."

"When was this?"

"In Laos. I guess it was in 1971. My father's friend, Lu Pham, called it Operation Lam Son. I'm not too familiar with the history of the war. But Mr. Pham said not giving my father's unit this information contributed to the failure of the whole operation."

During the war, Necaise had a college deferment and never served. He remembered Lam Son and how a few reporters considered it the turning point of the war. It was the time when America realized that the South Vietnamese could not support a sovereign country by themselves.

"My father eventually found out that the person who sabotaged his unit was the same officer who unjustly punished him for the crime Mr. Thompson had committed in Da Nang. Mr. Pham, who knew my father well, believes that my father would have considered the withholding of the information an act to punish him further. Therefore, in his mind, my father bore full responsibility for the casualties in his unit.

"Not only this, Agent Necaise, my father felt he contributed to the failure of Lam Son and the loss of American confidence in the South

Vietnamese. He felt responsible for Americans pulling out of the war. You see, intense feelings of guilt for the collapse of all South Vietnam burdened my father."

"No one man is responsible," Necaise said.

"No, not one man. Not just my father. But Mr. Pham told me that Father took full responsibility for his misdeeds, no matter how small. He was not angry at Mr. Thompson. He was angry at himself for the mistake he made in Da Nang and dishonored in his mind. For my father, integrity, honesty, and responsibility were inseparable from his spirit."

Anh opened the journal to the last page and pointed to her father's final handwritten entry. "Here, if I remember the translation correctly, he wrote this Vietnamese proverb, 'Those who eat salty fish will have to accept being thirsty.' You see what this means? He took complete responsibility."

"Your father appears to have been a great man," Necaise said.

"He was. I believe he struggled with guilt after the war. My mother said that he was angry at first with Mr. Thompson for starting the cascade of events that she knew of, and with time, he learned to forgive him. I don't think Mr. Thompson and Father harbored any lasting hatred toward each other. Mr. Thompson may not have liked the Vietnamese when he was younger. I don't think he feels that way now and is not a bad man. Mr. Thompson didn't kill my father. Before I told him this story, he knew nothing about what had happened to my father later in the war."

"You do know Rex Thompson confessed to the murder?" Necaise asked.

"Yes, I follow the news," Anh said. "We met just once, but I could tell he was sorry my father had died. I felt he had a deep sense of remorse. With your help, I would like to talk to Mr. Thompson again."

This request caught Necaise off guard. "What?"

"I want to talk to Mr. Thompson in jail."

"Miss Anh, it's highly irregular for the family of the victim to meet with the accused . . ."

"You don't believe he is guilty either," Anh said, taking a wild guess.

Necaise did not want to share his doubts about Rex Thompson, at least not now with Anh. An innocent man had confessed without coercion to a crime he did not commit. But for what reason? He had tried to get Rex to recant his confession but had failed. As Rex sat in jail, the actual killer, or killers, was free. Necaise looked at Anh; she had intense brown eyes and an unwavering stare. Her lips were drawn tight. She wore a tan overcoat tailored to her slight figure, buttoned and tied with a strap around her waist. How small she was, Necaise thought, but how large was her resolve.

"Okay, I'll make arrangements, and we'll go together."

"To talk with Mr. Thompson?"

"Yes."

Anh pulled a copy of the transcribed journal from a black leather tote and handed it to Necaise; she did not have to explain what it was.

"My mother does not yet know about this."

He took the sheaf of papers with both hands and looked at her. He realized then that guilt, not anger, was the boil that had festered in Don for many years and had shaped Anh's childhood with force invisible to her but always present. A power, Necaise thought, that gave her strength.

• • •

"Jake Thompson? Emily Schaffer from the *Coast Sentinel*. Can I ask you a few questions?" She extended a cassette recorder toward Jake as he came out of a convenience store.

Emily Schaffer was in her mid-twenties and a recent graduate of the Ole Miss School of Journalism. She had flowing blonde hair, sky-blue eyes, and a pleasant smile which set off her mouth full of white teeth.

"Yeah," Jake said.

He had noticed the striking woman standing outside the store window before he came out, and it pleased him that she approached.

"Mr. Thompson, people are saying your father confessed to sinking the *Miss Anh* because he was trying to cover for someone else. Have you heard this?"

"Nope."

"So, you think he sank the boat?"

"Yeah, he said so."

"Why do you think your father did it?"

"Because he hated the Vietnamese coming over here and taking all the damn shrimp. Don Nguyen—ya know he's Vietnamese—took Dad's boat, so he sank it. They's a lot of bad blood between 'em two, Dad and that Mr. Don," Jake said as he roughly constructed a motive.

Jake let his eyes drift to the reporter's tight-fitting black slacks, which accented her shapely hips. He glanced at her short puffy white coat trimmed with a fake fur collar and tried to imagine the chest, which would balance the rest of her body.

"You think your father is guilty then?" Emily asked.

"He said he done it. I believe 'im."

"There are reports it would be almost impossible for one man to pull this off by himself. Attaching a cable to a propeller six feet underwater at night without help would be difficult. Do you think he had help?"

"No, he could do it."

"How's that?"

"I bet he done tied the cable to the anchor rode first then lowered himself onto the prop with the other end."

"Excuse me, anchor rode?" she asked.

"Yeah, rode. Us boatmen call a rope going to the anchor, a rode. He was used to diving to the prop to un-foul it. We all was," Jake said.

He stared at Emily, standing next to him. Her blonde hair was blowing into her face, and she kept pulling it back behind her ear with her left hand. He noticed she wasn't wearing a wedding band.

"How would he have attached the cable to the anchor rode?"

"Probably with a shackle."

Jake figured his dad remembered the cable and large threaded steel shackle kept under the house and would have noticed it missing. His dad most likely confessed that he used this to scuttle the boat. Jake didn't think he was saying anything his dad had not already said.

"A shackle? How does that work?"

Emily knew what a shackle was and how it worked. Today wasn't the first time she had feigned ignorance to extract details. She held the recorder up toward Jake's mouth and hoped she could get a decent recording despite the wind hitting the microphone.

"He would've looped the cable around the anchor rode. Then to connect the cable to itself, used a shackle, a piece of metal like this." Jake held out his thumb and forefinger in a *U-shape*. "And screwed a bolt across like this." Jake placed his other forefinger across the *U* and worked his finger back and forth to his amusement. "Like screwed it."

Ignoring the obscene gesture, Emily asked, "Are you saying he wouldn't have attached the shackle directly to the anchor rope?"

"No, he would've run the cable around the anchor rode and attached the loop back to itself with the shackle."

She recognized she had something but was not sure of its significance. Jake was more than forthcoming, almost arrogant. She smiled at him again and said, "Where were you that night, the night the *Miss Anh* sank?"

"Sleeping," Jake said.

"At home?"

"Damn skippy, we was, Pigeon and me, both." An uncomfortable feeling came over him. He assumed he was no longer a suspect, but still, he had to watch his words. "Listen, Miss . . ."

"Schaffer."

"Miss Schaffer, I can't talk no more. I gotta go." Jake reached over and lifted a bicycle leaning up against the side of the store.

"I'd like to talk to you again." Emily held out a business card. "Please call me if you can. I have more questions."

Jake took the card and held it up to his nose. He smelled her perfume on it and wanted to stay and keep talking. Maybe after this blows over, Jake would look her up and see if she felt the same chemistry.

"I'll call you," Jake said, then peddled away.

Emily turned to her coworker sitting in a white Ford Escort at the edge of the parking lot—he had watched the whole exchange with Jake and was ready to jump out of the car to intervene—and she gave him a thumbs up.

CHAPTER 27

October 19, 1993

The phone rang. She answered, "Emily Schaffer, city desk."

"Miss Schaffer, Agent Necaise speaking, Mississippi Bureau of Investigation."

"Yes?"

"I read your piece in the paper this morning on Jake Thompson. I'm interested in what else Jake might have told you during your interview with him. If you have your conversation on tape, I want a copy."

Emily sat with the phone to her ear, not saying a word. Sure, she still had the tape. But should she share it with the police? What would her editors say? Wasn't it the job of a journalist to stay neutral and not divulge sources or methods? Obviously, the origin of the story was Jake; she had quoted him by name. Agent Necaise could only want the recording to search for anything Jake had said, which she left out of her story, or use his voice as evidence.

Emily didn't think Rex Thompson could have pulled the stunt off by himself, and she thought Jake was lying. If Jake and his brother had killed Don Nguyen, she would like to see them held accountable. Emily had known Timmy and Anh for a long time and wanted them to have justice.

"I'll have to get back to you, Agent Necaise. I really don't know if I can release it."

"I understand. Please call me later."

The dial tone hummed in her ear as she thought about Anh.

• • •

Rex expected Agent Necaise to be in the interrogation room, but not Anh. The Biloxi police officer who had escorted him from the county jail guided him into the room. Rex motioned with his chin to the handcuffs on his wrists and the chain around his orange jumpsuit.

"The cuffs stay on," the officer said. Rex had been polite to him on the way over from the jail. The officer resisted the return courtesy.

"Agent Necaise and Miss Anh," Rex said. He nodded his head in recognition, then sat with the help of the officer.

The policeman looked at Necaise, then left the room and closed the door. He would remain outside.

"I didn't know you'd be here today," Rex said, looking at Anh and trying to gauge her presence.

"Mr. Thompson," Necaise said, "I brought Anh Truong here today to speak to you."

"It's nice to see you again, Miss Anh. You know y'all don't need to waste your time with me."

Anh said, "Mr. Thompson—"

"Miss Anh, you—"

"Please, Mr. Thompson," Necaise interjected, "hear us out."

Rex knew why Necaise brought him over to talk. He knew there were cracks in his made-up story, and he would try to get him to recant his confession. Rex was ready to defend his statement. But having Anh in the room was a card he hadn't expected Agent Necaise to play.

"Mr. Thompson, I do not believe you were involved with sinking the boat that killed my father," Anh said. "When we met before, I saw in your eyes and heard from your lips you were innocent."

"You're wrong. Your father hated me, and I hated him," Rex said.

"No, that's not true. I saw tenderness and love. Not hate."

No sense arguing with this young lady, Rex thought. It didn't help him to speak at this point; Agent Necaise already had his admission of guilt.

"Mr. Thompson, as long as you remain in jail or prison for that matter, my family will not receive justice for the murder of my father. Do you understand me?"

Of course, he did, Rex thought. But what could this girl know of a wasted life like his, a life of poor choices, deceit, drunkenness, and ruin? What did she know of the love a father has for his sons, no matter their actions? Nothing. What did she know of the guilt a father feels when he has failed his children?

Rex asked Anh, "Does your mother love ya?"

"Sure, but—"

"Does your mother love you always? She'd love ya to the ends of the earth?"

"Yes."

"She would do anything for ya, keep ya from harm. Right?"

"She would, Mr. Thompson, but this is not about me—"

"It was painful for me to think that my sons couldn't, you know, use my boat after I lost it. I couldn't stand the thought of 'em watching it work the Sound with someone else at the helm. They shouldn't have to be reminded every day that their father screwed up, and the bank took the boat. Miss Anh, I sank it to protect my sons. . . . Sorry about your father. No, I didn't hate him. Don't know what he felt about me, but I didn't hate him. Didn't mean for no one to drown. That part was an accident. I wish I could take it all back. But I'm ready to serve my time," Rex said. "Look, I'm a criminal." Rex held up his cuffed hands as high as the waist chain permitted.

"Mr. Thompson," Necaise said. "I have evidence that says you didn't commit the crime."

"Y'all wrong," Rex said.

"You told a convincing story of how you scuttled the boat, dropping to the prop and all. But you got one detail wrong. Your son, Jake, the one who actually attached the cable to the anchor line with the shackle, got it right. I have the tape."

Rex had no response. He looked at Necaise, knowing that he was at a fork in the road, a decision point for the rest of his life.

"If you go to prison for this murder, you not only deny Mr. Nguyen's family justice, you deny your sons. Your sons know you're innocent. Locked up, you deny them a chance to see their father as a noble and honest man. You can't teach them integrity from prison."

An image appeared in Rex's mind. He was running in a sodden green lawn that squished with each footfall. Jake was at his heels, tugging on his shirt, squealing. Pigeon, sitting on his shoulders, had little arms wrapped tightly around his forehead. Water from Pigeon's wet white underwear dripped down his back. Round and round, they ran in the yard, under fruit trees, around lawn chairs, circling a blue plastic baby pool. In the water, floating with a red toy ship and several brown grass clippings, was a single cigarette butt—rose-colored lipstick smeared the filtered end.

"You can't be prosecuted for the theft in Da Nang," Necaise said. "That statute of limitations has run out." Necaise stood and paced the room, back and forth.

"I forgive you, Mr. Thompson," Anh said, "for what you did in the war, for what led to my father's pain. I can't forgive you for what you're doing right now."

Anh's words were piercing. Rex knew she was right; he denied them justice. It was time to stop this charade. He had been running his whole life, never owning up to the responsibility. This pretense was just another dodge of the truth, preventing him from reconciling his true feelings about his sons. Necaise was right. If he were to positively impact Jake and Pigeon, the time to start was now.

Rex looked at Necaise after a prolonged silence and asked, "Can I visit 'em in prison?"

Necaise stood still. He knew he had to proceed with caution at this moment. It was time to carefully peel back the layers of Rex's hardened emotional defenses and try to preserve something of his fragile core.

"Yes," Necaise said. "If they're guilty, you will have plenty of time to show your sons what a good father does."

"How long do you think they'll get?"

Necaise stepped in front of Rex and leaned forward on the table. "I don't know, but I hope long enough for them to heal and not a day longer."

"I don't know if they'll love me," Rex said.

"We can control only the love we bestow," Anh said. "I think, with time, your sons will come to appreciate this as well."

Rex Thompson slumped in his chair with his head low as if studying the white Converse tennis shoes on his feet. He looked up to Anh, sitting a mere three feet from him, and saw again in her eyes what he had seen when he met her once before, forgiveness and love. How could there be love in this room filled with hate, lies, and deceit? How could she find mercy for someone like him? Could he find it as well? A calming sensation then permeated his mind and body.

Rex looked over at Agent Necaise and said, "Okay."

"Anh, please excuse yourself and step outside," Necaise said. "Tell the officer to come in. I think Mr. Thompson has had a change of heart."

CHAPTER 28

October 24, 1993

The sound of tires rolling down the drive in the late afternoon caught Jake's attention. The sun was low in the western sky, casting a yellow hue over the woods surrounding the camp. Jake expected this visit from the police. As the cruisers approached, he slipped out the bedroom window with the Ruger .357 in his hand and two boxes of ammunition in a bag slung over his shoulder. Jake was ready. He had a plan.

The police had valid information that Jake was alone at the camp. They had already found Pigeon and Amber in Florida but had not yet taken them into custody. Because the officers assumed Jake was armed and would resist capture, a judge had issued a no-knock warrant for his arrest.

A ram breached the camp's front door, and four officers swarmed in to find the place vacant. They concluded that Jake had recently left on foot and must still be in the immediate area. The officers regrouped in the clearing around the house to set up a perimeter. Lieutenant Reilly called in surveillance teams to watch the surrounding access roads while six officers formed a squad and fanned out to search the adjacent woods.

Three hundred yards away, from his hole in a muddy ditch which drained tidal water into the bay, Jake was close enough to hear the rupture

of his front door. He lay prone against the bank facing the house. He smeared mud on his face and in his hair and covered his body with palmetto fronds. Unless they brought out the dogs, he thought, they would never find him.

The police officers spread out from the camp, looking for footprints and other signs of recent travel through the woods. Matted leaves and pine needles covered the ground. Wax myrtle, yaupon holly, and saw palmetto obscured the line of sight, limiting visibility into the brush to fifty yards. The police worked in a radial pattern, covering an ever-enlarging zone around the house.

Jake watched two officers emerge in a clearing seventy-five yards away then disappear. He could hear their muffled voices speaking over the radio. Frigid water seeped through Jake's shoes and clothing as he sank into the dark mud. A few weeks prior, he had seen a water moccasin in this ditch, and the thought of another encounter with the snake entered his mind and made him shudder.

Thirty minutes passed, and Jake remained hidden. The sun dropped below the horizon. Soon darkness would fill the woods under the dense canopy, allowing him to stay undetected and eventually slip the manhunt. Walls were closing in on him, and the prospect of arrest for the murder of Don Nguyen had him scared. But Jake had no intention of giving up. He had a plan to make a run and get out of this mess.

He saw an officer jump over his ditch twenty-five yards away and sink up to his ankles in the mud on the far side.

"Dammit," the officer yelled as he pulled himself out by grabbing hold of a low-hanging branch.

It wouldn't be long before the police surrounded him, Jake thought. He checked the load of his revolver and pulled back on the hammer. The beam of a flashlight scanned the water's edge to his left. The night was coming.

The officer backtracked across the ditch toward the house, picking his way through the brush with his light. A few more minutes, Jake thought, and he could make his break. Then he heard dogs baying and barking with excitement near the house.

Springing from the ditch, Jake ran away from the house and parallel to the shore. Saw palmetto thorns tore at his clothes and brushed against his face and neck. Jake found a path leading to his neighbor's property. He sped through the woods.

At the edge of a clearing, Jake scanned a raised camp much like his own. A dim light shone through thin curtains from a lone window at the back of the house. There were no police in the yard.

Jake knew the old man who lived there kept a runabout tied up to his dock with the ignition key hooked on a nearby post. The pier was dark, but Jake could see the twenty-foot boat's outline against light bouncing off the water's surface from the far shore of the bay. He made a run for the dock, grabbed the key, untied the boat, and jumped in. Jake lifted a boat hook from the deck and pushed the craft out into the water.

The barking of dogs got closer. Jake could see flashlights sweep the shore and woods halfway back to where he had hidden in the ditch. His scent would lead the dogs to the dock, his escape route detected. Headlights came down the drive, around the corner of the old man's camp, and lit up the surrounding yard. Jake fired up the outboard and pulled the throttle on the center console into gear. The back of the runabout pitched into the water as Jake spun the boat out toward the open bay. He watched the silhouettes of dogs and men, illuminated by car lights from behind, scurry about the dock as he raced away across the smooth surface of the water.

Jake turned up the channel and was soon past the Back Bay Bridge and heading up the Biloxi River. Adjusting to the near darkness, his eyes followed the meandering waterway through the tidal marsh. The banks narrowed on the river. He worked his way upstream to the interstate highway bridge. On the overpass sixty feet above, the blue flashing lights of several police cars cut shadows of men at the railing. His running lights were off, but he knew that anyone on the bridge could see and hear the little boat on the calm water below.

Beyond the highway bridge, brush and trees hung over the waterway, and the bayou narrowed to twenty feet. Jake saw no other boat on the water. It was impossible to follow him up the river without one. Few roads gave access to this part of the coast.

Jake pulled the boat into a narrow man-made channel three miles upriver, leading sixty feet to an abandoned barn. He had found this place years ago by accident. A perfect spot to hide if ever needed, he had thought at the time. Twenty feet square, the barn was clad in weathered vertical boards and roofed in corrugated sheet metal. It sat in a small clearing by itself. An overgrown, dirt drive curved up to a seldom-used country road just beyond the surrounding trees.

The runabout slid up to the muddy bank. Jake hopped out and tied it to a tree. He pulled dead branches over the boat. The crown of a dense oak covered the channel and made the runabout invisible from the air. Jake scrambled across the yard, entered the abandoned barn, and climbed up a ladder to its loft. At this point, his contingency plans ended. He would rest and figure out his next move later. Jake placed the gun and ammo by his side and lay on the rough planks in darkness.

At first light, the sound of cars traveling the nearby road woke him. He had slept little during the night.

The loft spanned the top of the barn. A small hay door faced the dirt drive and yard out front. Through gaps between the vertical planks covering the back wall, Jake could see the boat tied at the end of the narrow channel. Dense brush and trees blocked his view of the river and hid the barn from any passing boat.

His mouth was dry; hunger pains gripped his stomach. If he were to stay in his hideout for any time, he had to find some freshwater. A brackish, high tide had filled the lower river rendering it undrinkable. Perhaps standing rainwater in a nearby puddle or barrel could sustain him. He could tolerate not having food, but he knew he would not last more than a few days without water. He had no immediate plan to escape but was sure something would present itself.

The unmistakable sound of an airboat going up the river broke the quiet. Its airplane engine, driving a six-foot propeller mounted on the back of a flat-bottomed sled-like boat, gave off an unmuffled roar. An airboat nearby could only mean the police were searching for him on the river. Still, Jake felt confident the underbrush concealed the runabout, and his hideout was safe.

Jake dropped down the ladder from the loft and poked around the barn. The dirt floor was empty except for a few stray boards and two steel tire rims. Jake used one of the beams to slip through two rusted metal cleats on the inside of the barn doors. He then lifted the wheel rims to the platform, laid them across the hay door facing the road, and waited.

Sinking the *Miss Anh* had been his idea; Pigeon had followed the plan with ease. Jake had no intention of killing anyone. He knew the boat would settle to the shallow bottom of the bay. Anyone onboard could crawl up the rigging or onto the top of the pilothouse roof.

Jake was sure he and Pigeon could have beaten the rap if only Pigeon had kept quiet; if only their dad hadn't come back from wherever, confessed to the crime, and drawn more attention to themselves; and if Pigeon hadn't run.

Now, he was in a shit sandwich, he thought. Jake lay behind the rims, spun the barrel of his revolver, and looked toward the road.

The sound of the airboat came closer, passed upstream, then quit. Jake heard a small outboard motor idling on the river nearby. He crawled to the back of the barn, peeked through the boards, and looked to the channel. Nothing moved. The outboard engine sped up, and its sound traveled downstream.

Jake crawled back behind the steel rims and watched the driveway on the far side of the yard. He heard a car on the adjacent road. There was more action around him than he had expected. It was useless now to make a foot run. He had nowhere to go. Moving a boat up or down the river without being seen in full daylight was impossible. Jake decided to stay put. The search effort would move on, he reasoned. He would try to make a break tonight, jack a car, and get to the interstate.

Jake saw a police cruiser appear at the far side of the clearing and creep toward the barn. The car moved slowly down the drive. Jake crouched in the hay door behind the rims. He fingered his revolver and watched the car pull up below where he hid. Jake saw two cops in the front seat scanning the barn and the surrounding yard. Soon the boat would be discovered.

Jake pulled back on the hammer and aimed at the driver. The sound of his gun was deafening; the windshield spidered as the bullet hit its mark. The driver slumped sideways in his seat. The other officer jumped from the passenger side and rolled under the carriage. Jake fired off five rounds at him then stopped to reload.

The driver didn't move. Jake couldn't see the other man. It was quiet. Had he hit both cops? The sound of the airboat then broke the silence. Jake heard the boat race downstream and stop just on the other side of the trees, separating the barn from the river.

Movement at the far end of the clearing caught Jake's eye. A figure darted in the shadows. Jake scrambled to the back wall again, looking between the vertical boards at the channel and towards the river. Nothing.

Thoughts of death gripped him. He wanted it all to end. Could he toss his weapon and surrender? A second police car appeared in the drive, fifty yards away. Two officers jumped out and took up positions behind their vehicle. Jake aimed at the cruiser and shot four times, shattering the windshield and driver's side window. The roar of the airboat pounded in his ears. Jake saw someone move through the woods behind him. In a panic, he shot twice at the back wall of the barn.

Jake looked below the front opening and spotted the cop under the patrol car. He reloaded his gun, fired, and missed. Just then, burning pain shot through his left lower leg, followed by a rifle's report. Jake fell to the floor. Blood flowed from a baseball-size hole in the back of his pants. He looked at his leg, bent below the knee at an unnatural angle. He had no control of his ankle or foot. Game over, he thought. Another searing pain tore through his right shoulder and chest before the crack of the rifle met his ears.

Jake tossed his revolver out the window. He rolled to his back, looked up to the rafters and the underside of the metal roof, and coughed up blood. Moments later, he heard the ground door open and officers' voices enter the barn.

Extreme pain radiated from his left leg. When he tried to breathe, sucking and gurgling sounds came from his chest. His focus twisted on the rusting steel above him. He sensed someone was climbing the loft's ladder but could not lift his head to look. The barn went dark. The last things Jake sensed before losing consciousness were the muffled sounds of yelling. Were they yelling at him?

• • •

The Santa Rosa County sheriff picked up Pigeon and Amber at a mobile home park in Florida, a hundred miles east of Biloxi. The couple gave no resistance to arrest. The sheriff transferred both to the Biloxi police, who brought them back to Mississippi. The cops booked Pigeon on murder, attempted murder, sabotage of a vessel, possession of a controlled substance, and other felonies. They charged Amber as an accessory to the same.

• • •

"Take a deep breath," someone said, a lady perhaps. Jake felt a shake of his shoulder. A steady beep rang in his ears. It sounded like someone's heart tones. Jake struggled to open his eyes against a bright fluorescent light above. His left leg burned with excruciating pain.

"Mr. Thompson," the nurse said with a flat, business-like voice. "You're waking up from surgery. Take a deep breath."

Jake lifted his head from the pillow and looked around. He was not sure what he was seeing or where he was. To his right and left were purple curtains. He lay in a bed with chrome rails on each side. Past the foot of the bed, through an opening in the curtain, he could see people's heads on the far side of a high counter. A young woman in a white smock stood next to him with a syringe in her hand. She injected something into the clear tubing that led to his elbow.

"I'm giving you some more morphine to help with pain," she said.

Jake felt a warm rush in his head. His eyes rolled back, and the heart tones faded.

"Wake up, Mr. Thompson," the woman said. She poked him in the arm. "The doctor is here to speak to you."

Jake opened his eyes and noticed a short, wiry man with a gray crew cut and green scrubs at the foot of his bed. The young woman in the white smock pulled a blanket off his legs. Damn, his left leg was killing him, he thought.

The man in green spoke, "I'm Doctor Evans. I'm the surgeon who operated on your leg. Another surgeon put tubes in your chest where a bullet pierced your lung. He'll see you later about that."

Jake looked at the woman in the white smock. He thought she had the loveliest face, with deep brown eyes set wide above high cheekbones. She had pulled her chestnut hair back, showing her long slender neck. It felt as if she were touching his arm and tenderly holding his wrists.

". . . lost a large amount of blood. You're lucky to be alive. The bullet . . ."

The woman wiped his mouth with a white cloth and adjusted the pillow under his head. Jake tried to lift his hands to his face, but they were bound to the bed. "What the . . ." Light blue straps held his wrists.

"I couldn't save your leg."

Jake studied the man in green standing at the foot of the bed, wondering how long he had been standing there and what he was saying. Jake looked at a bandage on his left knee. He struggled to lift his leg, and pain shot up to his spine. He glanced at his other leg. A white stocking covered his right foot and felt tight around his calf. He noticed a metal cuff on his ankle. A short chain led to the bed rail. "What the hell?" He tried to refocus on the woman and the man standing at his bed.

". . . the entrance wound was just below the knee. The bullet hit your tibia, your shin bone. The bullet shattered the bone, sending sharp fragments into the soft tissue of your lower leg. Are you understanding this?" the surgeon asked.

"Yeah, Doc." Jake nodded.

"Okay. I opened the wound and explored your nerves and arteries. Your tibial nerve was . . ."

Jake closed his eyes. His left leg throbbed. "Git me somepin for pain," he said, assuming the woman in the white smock was still at his side.

"I just gave you something. Relax. Listen to the doctor."

". . . the arteries were destroyed as well, and you were getting no blood to your foot. There was too much damage to be able to repair. I had to amputate your leg below the knee."

But his left ankle and foot screamed in pain. How could this be? Jake opened his eyes again and lifted his head from the pillow. He looked at the surgeon and tried to concentrate. What a little man, Jake thought. *Little big man.*

"I removed the part that the rifle bullet destroyed. I left as much as I could."

"What the fuck?" Jake's mind suddenly cleared. "Y'all didn't fucking cut my leg off?"

"Yes, I just got through explaining this to you."

"Git me the fuck out of here," Jake screamed at the nurse in the white smock. "You're a bunch of got-damn butchers." Jake twisted his body in the bed but couldn't sit up or roll. The restraints held his wrists. "Git these got-damn things off my arms," he barked.

Jake tried to pull his right leg up to kick, and he felt the pinch of the shackle at his ankle. He looked at his other leg and saw that a stain of blood had soaked through the bandage where his lower leg should have been.

"Five more milligrams of Valium," the doctor said to the nurse before he walked out of the recovery room to speak with the police.

CHAPTER 29

November 22, 1993

Linh stood in her bedroom doorway. "Thi Anh, can I speak to you?" she said to her daughter.

"*Vâng.*" Anh nodded, put down her book, and followed her mother to the back room. Much had happened in the past several weeks since Rex Thompson's arrest and his later release from jail, the shootout between Jake and the police, and the eventual capture of Pigeon and Amber. Every day in the local paper, Linh and Anh read the developing case against the two brothers. They learned from the evening news how the Biloxi police officer, who Jake had shot in the abdomen, survived after being flown by helicopter to the University Hospital. Each story in the paper or on the TV caused Anh and Linh to relive Don's tragic drowning. Through self-preservation or fatigue, Anh and Linh stopped talking about the incident, and with time, stopped talking much to each other.

"Thi Anh, please sit," Linh said as she stood next to her bed.

Anh loosened her robe and sat on the simple spread which covered the full-sized bed her parents used to share. The room was familiar to her. She looked at a tarnished brass lamp with a yellowing shade on a small rosewood nightstand. On the table was her father's gold watch—the one he wore to church and never would have taken on the boat. The timepiece no longer ticked; its second hand, still. Anh glanced at her mother's dresser—also rosewood—and the large mirror mounted to the back. Dark-red rosary beads with a tarnished silver cross hung from the top of the mirror as if reminding the one reflected to follow their faith daily. Anh knew it was not her mother's only rosary. She kept more in her nightstand beside her bed.

Linh walked over to a tall, triangular curio cabinet in the corner of the room. She opened the glass door and removed a small porcelain statue from the top shelf.

"My mother gave this to me when I was a young girl," Linh said as she handed the figurine to Anh.

Anh had seen this three-inch statue at the top of the curio for as long as she could remember. It was part of the room and always present. Her mother had never taken it down, and Anh had never held it in her hands.

She was stunning, Anh thought. The statuette was of a lady with a light blue robe and a gold halo around her head. She held a dark-haired infant in a red gown—the Virgin Mary with the Christ Child.

"*Đức Mẹ La Vang,*" Linh said, "Our Lady of La Vang."

Anh handled the figurine and admired the smooth white enamel on Mary's face and the gold trim of her robe. Baby Jesus sat upright in her arms and faced forward with his right hand raised in a gesture of peace. The Virgin and her Son were delicate and finely made.

"This was the only thing, besides you and the clothes on my back, that I brought with me from Vietnam when we escaped," Linh said. "Remember, today is the Feast of Our Lady of La Vang?"

"Yes, Mother."

"I should have gone to mass. You should have gone to mass. I have so much to confess, and my heart is heavy, burdened. I pray for forgiveness."

"You have done nothing wrong, Mother."

"Impure thoughts can be as sinful as deeds. I have had many of these in the past few months. I need to pray more. Nevertheless, I never fail to remember Our Lady on this day. It is right you should have her today."

"She's yours. I couldn't, Mother."

"Nonsense. I have always intended for you two to stay together. She belongs to you even more than me." Linh sat on the bed and tenderly placed her palm on Anh's belly, hoping to feel movement. She smiled at her daughter, then pulled her hand away.

"After you were born, and your father was missing in Laos, I did not know if he was alive or dead. I prayed to *Đức Mẹ La Vang* every day for his safe return."

"Where were you?"

"Near Quang Ngai, staying with your great-aunt on the coast."

Anh held the porcelain figure up to the light to study a small inscription on its base.

Linh continued, "You know, many Vietnamese Catholics worship Our Lady of La Vang. We believe she will answer your prayers if you are sick, hurting, lost, or lonely. We are Catholic because my parents were Catholic, and their parents before them. The Dominicans and the Jesuits brought Christianity to our country many years ago. Did you know it's not always been easy for Christians in Vietnam? They suffered much persecution."

Anh shook her head.

"Many years ago, in the 1700s, a group of Christians sought refuge from an emperor in the rainforest of Quang Tri, north of Quang Ngai. They became ill. Every night they gathered under three trees to pray. One night a lady's image appeared to them in the branches. She wore a traditional dress, held an infant, and had two angels at her side. The people recognized her as the Blessed Virgin Mary.

"Mary comforted the people gathered and told them to collect a particular leaf and make a tea to cure their disease. A miracle happened in the jungle mountains of La Vang. Many pilgrims traveled there to worship. Eventually, they built a shrine, then a basilica."

"Have you been there?" Anh asked.

"Yes, and so have you, when you were only seven months old."

Today was the first time Anh had heard her mother tell of this.

"It had been many months since your father disappeared. Nobody could tell me his whereabouts or if he was even alive. I put my faith into *Đức Mẹ La Vang*, but my prayers were not answered. I knew I had to go to the Basilica of La Vang myself."

"But the war?" Anh asked.

"It was not smart, I know. But at the time, I felt I had no choice. I guess I had more faith than common sense. My uncle had a motorbike, and I convinced him to take the two of us to La Vang."

"You, we, rode a motorbike?"

"Yes, we rode at night without lights and with you strapped to my back. We took small roads and dirt paths between fields. My uncle had lost an eye and left hand in the war, so he balanced his wrist on the handlebar and held a leather strap in his teeth to pull the clutch. La Vang was three hundred kilometers away. It took three nights to get there. During the day, we hid and rested. Many times, while on the road, we concealed ourselves in a ditch or behind a bush to avoid detection. We had no authorization to travel. Had we been discovered, the soldiers would have us arrested."

"But, were you still in South Vietnam?" Anh asked.

"Yes, it didn't matter. There was a war with a general curfew. Where we were heading was near the Demilitarized Zone between the North and South."

Anh had never thought of her mother as adventurous or brave. Her tale of this journey was hard to believe.

"The first night, we rode through rice paddies and along narrow paths that ran the tops of levees, separating the fields. The moon was out. I remember how lovely the paddies looked with the moonlight's reflection, softened by the young rice stalks, on the water's surface. By morning, we made it to the Tra Kieu Shrine on the Thu Bon River bank, just south of Da Nang. We hid among the ruined ramparts in an ancient city where there was a church. That day, I believe Our Lady of Tra Kieu protected us from harm.

"Just after dark on the second night, we headed north on dirt paths and made our way past Da Nang. I could see the airfield with bombers and jets taking off and landing. Planes flew so low and close I thought they would blow us off the motorbike. I covered your little ears and eyes with my hands while the jets passed.

"Soon, we came to a mountain range running east to the sea. There were no safe roads or trails across the hills, so we had to head to the coast. Because all roads went through a bottleneck, this section of the journey was most treacherous. My uncle was nervous and wanted to turn back. I accused him of cowardice, and on we pressed. Eventually, we reached the Perfume River outside Hue City. The river was wide and deep. Soldiers guarded the bridges, and we could not cross. The morning light was showing in the sky to the east, so we found refuge for the day within the walls of the Tu Duc Tomb."

"What did you eat?" Anh asked.

"We had dried fish and rice cakes I had packed."

"And sleep?"

"Only mats on the ground. I could not think of hunger or discomfort, for I thought only of your father. If he were alive, he was suffering much more than I."

Linh continued, "The tomb in which we hid was made for an ancient emperor; it was very tall and decorated with orange tiles. Stone statues of elephants and dragons guarded the entrance gates and staircases. As the sun rose, light entered the vault's large arches and made the tomb glow like a lantern. I had never seen such a beautiful thing. One day I hope you can visit the tomb yourself."

"Yes, I would like that, Mother." Anh rolled the statuette in her hands.

"By evening, my uncle had found a man with a raft who agreed to ferry us across the river. That night, when I saw that the raft was just a collection of small logs lashed together with vines, I hesitated. I could not swim. If the raft tipped, then you and I would have drowned in the deep muddy water. As we paddled out into the river, the craft listed severely to the side and threatened to capsize. I apologized to my uncle for asking him to take us on such a journey. I thought we were to die that night. *Đức Mẹ La Vang*, however, watched over us; she had other plans for our lives. We made it safely to the north bank with the motorbike and continued.

"By this time, we were only sixty kilometers from La Vang. My uncle drove into farmland and followed cart paths through fields of cassava and sweet potato. In one of these dark fields, we came upon a man who jumped from behind a tree. He leveled a rifle at my uncle's chest and demanded to know our business. My uncle and I were no threat to this man. By his accent and dress, I guessed he was a farmer. We did not know if he sympathized with the Vietcong. Right away, you started to cry out loud and made a commotion altogether. My uncle said, 'The baby is sick. We must see a doctor.' The man lifted his rifle and allowed us—a one-eyed, one-handed old man, a young mother, and a wailing infant—to pass.

"The three of us made it to the Basilica of Our Lady of La Vang just after midnight. The moon came up over the horizon and lit up the old white stone church, which loomed high above a large open field surrounded by jungle. A silent bell tower stood above the entrance, supporting a large cross on its roof. I remember thinking the cross and church seemed to stand as a testament to the Christian faith in the South against the atheist Communists just across the border to the north.

"We entered the sanctuary through a side door and found the altar by crawling on our hands and knees in near-complete darkness. With you in my arms, I knelt and prayed. I prayed to *Đức Mẹ La Vang* for you. I prayed for your father. I prayed for the end of the war. And I cried.

"Thi Anh, in my sleeve was this little figurine you are holding now. That night in the church, I pulled it out, placed it in your little hands, and held them with my own. I prayed again."

Linh then cupped her hands over Anh's and the statue of the Virgin Mary. Tears streamed down Anh's cheeks. She could not speak.

"*Đức Mẹ La Vang* eventually answered my prayers, and your father returned to us two months later. The North Vietnamese bombed the Basilica of La Vang the day your father came home. The bombing destroyed all but the bell tower. The spirit of *Đức Mẹ La Vang,* however, lives on in the hearts of many Vietnamese."

Linh released Anh's hands, and Anh wrapped her arms around her mother's shoulders. Anh glanced at the mirror above the dresser and could see her mother's back and neck reflected. She could also see the image of the little statue of Our Lady of La Vang, clenched in her hand and partially obscured by the hanging rosary beads. Anh tightened her embrace.

Minutes passed before Anh released her mother and placed the statuette on the nightstand next to her father's wristwatch. Now, she had many questions for her mother, questions she had never thought to ask. Most pressing were questions about her father.

"Do you know if Father brought anything with him from Vietnam?" Anh was testing. Did her mother know of the cloth insignia, ribbon bar, or journal?

"Nothing," Linh responded. "He had some gold he used to help us escape, but that was gone."

"When we took the boat?" Anh asked.

"Yes, that is a story for another day."

Anh had thought much about the journal. Should she share this with her mother? Obviously, her mother knew the history of her father's youth, early military career, and time at Da Nang. She had previously told Anh the overall story of his capture and imprisonment. But, in the journal, her father had also written about the colonel who withheld information from the 1st Armored Brigade. Anh suspected her mother knew nothing of the guilt her father shouldered for Lam Son's failure and the negative shift in the war. Anh was sure her mother did not know that her father carried this burden for the rest of his life. Anh was sorry she ever found the hidden box; its contents raised many more questions than answers. Would it serve any useful purpose now to reveal the journal to her mother?

"Mother, would you stay right here? I have something to show you." Anh slipped out of the bedroom for a moment. When she returned, she held out the insignia and ribbon bar in her hands for her mother to see. "I found these in a small box in the outside locker."

"I don't understand."

"I showed them to *Chú* Lu, and he told me what they were. I can only assume they belonged to Father. You have never seen these?"

"No. Are they from the war?"

"Yes, *Chú* Lu said this one is the rank of lieutenant colonel." Anh handed over the small green patch of cloth with two embroidered silver blossoms above a gold bar.

"But he was a captain."

"No, I think Father must have obtained this rank before the war ended."

"He never said a word of this," Linh said.

"Does it seem odd that Father would hide this from you?"

"No, he kept much to himself."

"But this was a significant promotion for him."

"I don't know why."

Anh then gave her mother the red and yellow military ribbon. "This is the National Order of Vietnam; Father was a hero."

"National Order?"

"Yes, I looked it up. This was South Vietnam's highest military honor. Did he say nothing of this to you?"

"No."

"Never told you he did something heroic in the war?" Anh asked.

"No, Anh. Your father spoke little of what he did in the war. I know he fought bravely in Quang Tri and Hue. But he never mentioned an award to me."

"He never told you about being promoted?"

"I didn't see him in the last three years of the war. When he finally found me, the country was collapsing, and he was wearing peasant's clothing. Our army was falling apart. We left immediately by boat."

Anh now saw her father in a new light. She saw a man who assumed full responsibility for a minor mistake in Da Nang. An error that snowballed into a massive disaster on the Se Pone River. Anh guessed her father fought with courage in the last two years of the war to compensate for the dishonor he had brought upon himself in Da Nang. His valor might have eased his guilt but never erased his shame or merited recognition in his mind. Anh was sure this was why her father hid the journal, rank, and ribbon. Perhaps he saved these mementos for the day when he could find peace within himself and share this part of his story with his family. That day never came.

Linh pressed the statue of Our Lady of La Vang and the cloth relics into Anh's palm. "Anh, your father was a great man. I know he did many great things that we will never understand. We don't need to know *what* these things were for us to know *who* he was."

Anh dried her eyes with her sleeve.

"Mother, I have one more thing to show you." Anh reached into her robe pocket and pulled out the small tan book. "I also found this."

CHAPTER 30

December 21, 1993

Rex Thompson walked from the waterfront along Myrtle Street to a shoofly, a raised deck surrounding a gigantic live oak trunk. Despite being the winter solstice, it was one of those warm, bright December days in Biloxi that tricked your mind into thinking spring was right around the corner.

Rex bounded up a flight of stairs to the whitewashed platform. He could see south over the coastal road to the Biloxi Bay, Deer Island, and the Sound from the top of the steps. The shoofly appeared empty. Were his time and date correct?

Rex moved to the north side of the octagonal deck and saw the shoulders and knees of a woman sitting on the inner bench with her back against the tree trunk. A green and red plaid blanket covered her lap. She was alone. Rex knew who she must be.

"Mr. Thompson?" she asked as she turned her head.

"Yes. Please call me Rex." He extended his hand, not sure if she would take it.

"I am pleased to meet you. My name is Thuy Linh Nguyen." She remained seated and took his hand in hers. "It would make me happy if you called me Linh."

"Linh. I was expecting Timmy and Anh today," Rex said, still holding Linh's hand. Her fingers were delicate; her grip was slight yet purposeful. "Timmy called."

"I know, but I wanted to talk to you alone."

Meeting Linh caught Rex off guard. He was not ready for what she might say. Rex had no doubt that Linh knew his entire story. Anh had said so herself. Of course, he was sorry for what he had done in Da Nang and sorry for the trouble this caused Don over the years.

She released his hand, and he sat facing Linh on a bench opposite her. Rex was about to speak when Linh said, "I forgive you, Mr. Rex."

"But—"

"Please listen to what I have to say." Linh clutched a Bible on her lap. Its black binding was worn by many hands, exposing light brown leather. Only a faint hint of gold leaf remained on the warped and curled edges of its thin pages.

Rex reached for his copy of the New Testament in his pants pocket. But the little book was no longer there. He had tossed it in the water the day he took to the skiff—the day he found the bottle again, the day he had lost hope and was buried in guilt.

"My husband survived the war with wounds you could not see," she continued. "He had holes of rage, vengeance, and shame in his body. You could not see these holes from the outside, but they were there."

"I'm sorry," Rex said.

"Please," she said. "My husband was a courageous and patriotic soldier in South Vietnam. He loved his country and committed to defending it against the communist enemy. He was always very thankful that America sent fighters like you to try to save our struggling nation."

Rex's thoughts shot back to his first tour in Bien Hoa. He looked at Linh—a *mama-san.* Then he was a twenty-one-year-old airman who had never traveled beyond South Texas, including boot camp in San Antonio. Once in Vietnam, all things foreign had filled his senses. New sights. New sounds. Nothing prepared him to enter a war halfway around the world where he couldn't distinguish an enemy from an ally. In Vietnam, Rex had reacted with bravado and talk of supremacy. *He would kick some gook-*

ass, pronto. But beneath the patina of toughness, he now knew, had been a frightened young man.

"At the end of the war, my husband understood that South Vietnam was fighting a lost cause. He did not blame the United States for leaving. When we came to this country in 1975, we were thankful for what the Americans had done for us."

Rex wasn't sure he had done much at all for South Vietnam. On both tours in the war, he had filled a seat and pushed papers. He had left Vietnam with contempt for its war, its culture, and its people.

"In America, we felt safe, and Dung thought he could heal the holes in his body and find peace. However, when you moved to Biloxi and Dung saw you for the first time since the war, his old wounds opened," Linh said.

"I didn't know."

"Of course, you didn't know. I didn't know much either. Long ago, Dung had shared with me the details of what happened between the two of you in Da Nang."

Rex was still unsure why he stole the money. Only in the past two months had he realized how much this single act affected so many people, especially Don. Was the theft also the catalyst for his own downfall?

"I was aware that Dung had been sent to fight in Laos and was taken a prisoner by the North. I learned later he was sent back to the frontlines and fought bravely for the last three years of the war. I thought he directed his continued anger only at you. I thought he blamed you for losing his job in Da Nang and for being sent to Laos. I urged him to forgive you and forget—to move on with his life."

"Wish I could undo what I'd done."

"You could not have anticipated the consequences then. Nobody could. Dung didn't either."

"But—"

"I didn't understand the full extent of my husband's anguish until just recently when I read the journal that Anh shared with you. You see, Dung was an immensely proud and private man. In his mind, he made the wrong choice in Da Nang in dealing with you, and this brought dishonor to himself and his family. This produced profound guilt. Then, learning that information was deliberately withheld because of him, as his brigade was trying to flee Laos, only magnified his guilt."

"That can't be true."

"I believe it was true in Dung's mind. So true, I believe now, that Dung spent the rest of the war in a gallant fight to overcome his shame. Despite acts of heroism unknown to me, he could never achieve repair of his honor. I know now that Dung felt partially responsible for the failure in Laos, which led to the gradual withdrawal of America, and eventually, the collapse of the South Vietnamese Army. You see, my husband, in his mind, felt responsible for the lives of hundreds of thousands of his countrymen."

"That's absurd," Rex said.

"Yes. But I'm sure, now, that is what he felt. It was an enormous burden he could not reconcile."

"But losing an entire war?"

"He never spoke of this to me. He internalized his guilt, and it turned into anger. This anger is what I saw. At that time, I did not understand the scope of his conscience."

Rex had studied the journal but missed the nuances in events that led Don to the conclusions that Linh was describing. It was clear to Rex he knew neither the history nor culture of Vietnam well enough to understand.

"I told Dung for many years that to find *peace,* he had to forgive. That is what the Bible says, doesn't it?"

"Yeah, it says that."

"It says in the Book of Matthew, 'If you forgive others their transgressions, your heavenly Father will forgive you.' I believe this, and, eventually, I think Dung did as well."

"I'm sorry, I . . ."

"Do you believe this about forgiveness?"

"Yes, I'd like to."

"Good. My husband wanted to tell you he forgave you. He tried many times to approach and tell you, but he couldn't. He needed to but couldn't. Is it enough to forgive someone and stay silent?" Linh asked without expecting an answer. "Must one accept an apology from another before one can forgive? 'If your brother sins, rebuke him; and if he repents, forgive him.'"

"Luke."

"Yes . . . Mr. Rex, I believe now my husband felt you could repent for stealing the money, but if you did not know the extent of the anguish which rippled out from that act, and you were not rebuked, then you could not repent and be forgiven, completely. He wanted to let you know what happened to him and his countrymen and give you an opportunity for complete salvation. But also, he felt he needed to do this for his own salvation as well. He drowned before he found the courage to speak to you. Thi Anh understood this, and that is why she shared Dung's journal with you."

"I'm so sorry for what I did in Da Nang," Rex said. "I have many regrets in my life, and this is one of the greatest. I ask you to forgive me."

"I told you I already have."

"I'm also sorry for raising sons who could do such a thing to your husband. I apologize for not being a better father to 'em. I didn't give 'em the guidance they needed. I failed . . ."

"Mr. Rex, we have a saying in our culture that translates like this 'Many a good father has but a bad son.' I take this to mean that our children are not only from us. Or, as one of your American prophets once wrote about our children, 'They are the sons and daughters of Life's longing for itself.' You need not apologize for the actions of your sons."

From his seat, Rex gazed toward the bay and the spot where the *Miss Anh* sank. Did Linh deliberately sit with her back to the water to force him to look beyond her and out to the Gulf? How dreadful the thought that the money he stole in Da Nang was used to buy the boat in which the man, who suffered most from his crime, had drowned. Oh, how he wished he could change the past.

"When my husband died, his burdens became mine," she said. "I felt anger inside me. I had not felt this before, a hole filled with hate. I had overcome hate and revenge many years before when I had forgiven you and everyone else, who had cast misery on our lives. But now, hate was back inside me. When I thought you murdered my husband, I hated you."

Linh looked at Rex, sitting just feet away. Tears welled up in her eyes. She took a small, laced kerchief from beneath her book and dabbed her cheeks. Rex noticed the same olive-shaped face, surrounded by thick jet-black hair, he had seen in her daughter. Linh had drawn her long hair back to a loose bun that sat at the top of her collar. Wrinkles lined her forehead and corners of her eyes as if the skin could not remember a time when worry and despair did not exist. Rex wondered if her thin lips could ever again stretch to a smile.

"Mr. Rex, I want to tell you, and for my husband's sake, both of us forgive you. I hope you can find a way to forgive me for hating you so much when I thought you killed him."

"You've done nothing wrong. You don't need to ask for forgiveness."

"But I have, Mr. Thompson, and I repent. In time, I hope to heal and forgive your sons as well."

Rex got up and sat on the inner bench next to Linh. From her viewpoint, he could see the homes and trees which covered her neighborhood on the Point. He saw children playing tag in the front yard of a house painted bright yellow and a corner store across the street. Out front was a red wagon tied to the back of a bicycle. Cars were driving down the main road through the neighborhood, going to work, school, church. Behind Linh and him was the past. Both were now looking toward the future.

"I forgive you, Mrs. Nguyen."

They both sat in silence under the shade of the live oak and watched a man with two young children come out of the corner store. The kids appeared to be two or three years old and held bright orange popsicles dripping to their elbows. The man placed both children and a bag of groceries into the red cart. He then mounted the bicycle and rode off with the wagon in tow.

Linh bowed her head, glanced for a moment at the deck of the shoofly, and smiled. She then looked up to Rex and said, by drawing out her vowels in a slight Southern accent, "Thank you."

CHAPTER 31

April 3, 1994

"Good morning," Nancy said.

Rex glanced up and noticed his friend standing in the aisle at his side. "Morning."

"May I?" Nancy gestured to the seat next to him, the last pew, back of the church.

"It's nice to see you. Oh, of course, sit. Please." Rex lifted a Missal and a bulletin, then wiped imaginary dust off the seat.

Nancy wore a floral print dress with a broad white lace collar draped out to the edge of her shoulders. She faced the altar, genuflected while making the sign of the cross from her forehead to chest, then eased herself into the pew. She flipped the kneeler with one hand and dropped to her knees.

Rex gazed at the back of her head and shoulders. A tortoiseshell barrette held her long brown hair neatly in place. He closed his eyes. He could smell the slight scent of her perfume. Rex listened to her faint breathing, interrupted as if she was mouthing the words to a prayer. He sensed her sitting back up in the pew, and he opened his eyes.

"Rex, what brings you to St. Michael's this morning?" she asked.

"Baptism." He held up the bulletin for her to see.

Rex had on a gray suit coat with black pants. A plastic nametag on his left breast pocket read SECURITY REX GALVESTON TEXAS.

"Oh, a baptism. I forgot that it was today. How nice."

Rex straightened his collar.

"Are you working at the casinos now?" Nancy asked while looking at his nametag.

"Yeah, across the street at the Azalea Queen."

"You're not bothered by temptation?"

"Sure, every day. Y'all know what they say about keeping your enemies close. I keep 'em all close. Gives me freedom."

"Good. . . . You know the baby?" Nancy asked, snapping the bulletin with her fingers.

"Sort of, I—"

A bell rang, and the congregation rose. Rex stood with Nancy and watched three acolytes, dressed in black and white robes, carry a brass cross and two large candlesticks down the central aisle. Deacons, lay ministers, and priests filed in behind the cross. Musical notes from an organ and voices from a choir—played and sung to the glory of God—filled the sanctuary.

The priest placed the Book of Gospels on the stone altar and said a few words Rex didn't entirely understand. The congregation responded with a booming, "Amen." Suspended from cables over the altar, a large bronze cross and wavy ring floated high in the nave. Easter lilies adorned the chancel.

Rex turned to Nancy and tried to continue his explanation of why he was here today. "I know the family."

She touched her left hand to his knee and brought her right forefinger up to her lips, "Shh."

Rex noticed her deep-red lipstick was the same color as the polish on her fingernails and the flowers of her dress. She smiled then clasped her hands together, intertwining her fingers and lining up her red nails like rubies on a crown. Rex returned his attention to the front of the church and watched the service proceed—a ceremony foreign to him. Song, prayer, song, readings, prayer, up, down, kneel and stand—he followed Nancy's lead and even anticipated an occasional *amen*.

Rex thought of Jake and Pigeon marking idle time at Parchman. He had not yet summoned the courage to drive north past Yazoo City into the Delta to visit them. At their trial, Necaise had worked out a deal with the DA so that he would not have to appear as a witness. The jury verdict—murder while committing a felony—was unanimous, and sentencing was dispensed with haste.

Rex gazed up to the narrow stained-glass windows that spanned from floor to ceiling, surrounding the circular sanctuary. In the openings, angular shards of colorful blue, red, and yellow glass depicted the Twelve Apostles as fishermen gathering their catch in nets—*Fishers of Men*.

Large hands pulled at the edges of a seine, teeming with fish. Colorful robes, pooling in shallow water, clung to the wet flesh of muscular bodies. Square geometric eyes looked back at him from all directions. Rex felt both comforted and condemned by the images.

Would the *Fishers of Men* ever have thrown back to the Sea of Galilee an unwanted fish, something like him, someone so unworthy of salvation? Or if caught, would he have resisted salvation and jumped from the boat? How many times in the past had he been pulled in by the nets and refused to stay? He reckoned he had had dozens of opportunities in his life to answer the call of the *Fishermen* but had declined. Only when he was sick and desperate did he turn to Jesus, and then just for a while. Thank God someone caught him one last time and brought him into His fold.

A burning question then surfaced in his mind: could he now be a *fisherman* for his own sons, the ones cast off?

In a large white vestment, the priest announced to the congregation that the baptismal party, and all little children who wished to see, should come forward to the square white font. Rex saw Timmy, Anh, Linh, and several other people gather around the priest from the back of the church. In Timmy's arms was a white silk gown draped halfway to the floor. Thick black hair on a tiny head rested in the crook of his elbow. Little hands grasped at the air. Anh peered at this bundle, smiled, and straightened out the dress so it hung gracefully off her husband's arms.

The priest looked at the people gathered around the baptismal font and asked so the entire congregation could hear, "What name do you give this child?"

"Dominic Truong Chuong Duy," Anh, Timmy, and Linh answered in unison.

Rex leaned over to Nancy and whispered, "They call 'im Donny."

Acknowledgements

I am indebted to my friend Cecil George Smith and the other Ocean Springs Writer's Guild members for their inspiration and encouragement as I kindled this story. Thank you, Richard Gollott, for bringing the Biloxi shrimping history to life through stories of your father.

And to the late Vietnam veteran and friend Russell Thompson, who was able to vividly recall after fifty years the sights, smells, and noise of *his* war, I am glad to have known you.

I am thankful for the sharp editing and plot hole filling of Valerie Winn, Susan Leon, Melissa Nick, and NancyKay Wessman. I appreciate Kim Tran, who taught me the subtle difference between her native translation for *massive boat fire* and *candle flame* and salvaged a hilarious mistake. To Robert Lindsey, Ramona Smith, Sherye Green, and Keith Stewart thank you for unselfishly pouring over early drafts of the manuscript and offering valuable critiques.

I am beholden to Mississippi journalist Trang Pham-Bui, who experienced the Vietnamese diaspora and generously offered observations on her culture's assimilation in America.

To all the staff at Touchpoint Press, especially Kim Coghlan, Ashley Carlson, and Sheri Williams, thank you for believing in this untested writer and making the best of this book.

Bycatch would never have come to fruition without the assistance of my sister Kathryn Freer and daughter Meghan Moore. They listened compassionately and repeatedly to all my writing fears and tribulations. But most important was the love and support of my wife, Marcia, without which this book would only be a dream.

CPSIA information can be obtained
at www.ICGtesting.com
Printed in the USA
JSHW020202261122
33720JS00007B/17

9 781956 851236